YOU KNOW THERE'S
SOMETHING

ALSO BY JOHN OLSON

YOU KNOW THERE'S
SOMETHING

JOHN OLSON

grand IOTA

Published by
grand**IOTA**

2 Shoreline, St Margaret's Rd, St Leonards TN37 6FB
&
37 Downsway, North Woodingdean, Brighton BN2 6BD

www.grandiota.co.uk

First edition 2023

Cover photo by Ahmed Fahmi on Unsplash
Typesetting & book design by Reality Street

A catalogue record for this book is available from the British Library

ISBN: 978-1-874400-89-9

You know there's something. Something silent. Something vaguely askew. Something buried and coming to the surface. Something breeding trouble. Something weirdly serene and rippling. Something wonderful. And it all comes due tomorrow and it all depends on you. And nothing about anything is normal or will be again.

I'm waiting, as always, to go somewhere. It's a feeling I like and dislike simultaneously. I like going places. It's exciting to go somewhere. Even if it's just a short ride to the grocery store. But I'm also quintessentially sedentary. I like the inertia I find in chairs and couches and beds. I can be still for hours at a time. I'd make a good coffee table. I can take a slice of life and ignite it with a mug of robusta. That would take me somewhere interesting for a few minutes. Sometimes you can go places without stepping out of the room. For example: *A Journey Around My Room*, by Xavier de Maistre. Or "The Mark on the Wall" by Virginia Woolf, a journey through a woman's mind. A lot of odysseys occur without benefit of airplane or automobile. They can happen when you're lying in bed, or gazing out the window on a rainy day, or looking at a map on the internet. I like it when I find a seat in the waiting area at the airport and can sit there with my luggage and relax a little. Also when the plane begins to board and you walk down that tunnel that hooks up to the door of the plane and nod hello to the flight attendants and shuffle awkwardly down the aisle and, finding your seat, sit down. The even-tempered tone of the pilot's voice coming over the loudspeaker. The long taxi to the end of the runway. The roar of the engines. The euphoria of leaving the ground. The calm of looking down at the city where, for a few minutes, and before clouds cover it all up, nobody's problems can seem all that big.

I get this way especially just before going for a run. This feeling of anticipation. My body perceives the efforts it's about to make and the exhilaration that will come with it. Weird to think I'm in my 70s and still running every day. I didn't think I'd be running at all this late in life. I was never particularly athletic. But here I am. Oriana asks if I have her peanuts and I say yes. We feed the neighborhood crows unsalted peanuts. We've gotten to know a few of them and have named them. Today is a short run, four miles. We have to stop by the library.

It's a little hotter than usual for the Pacific Northwest. I'm loving every minute of it.

As soon as I round the Desert Sun Tanning Salon (now gone), I feel a breeze on my back. It feels good. I've been sweating and the large awning covering the sidewalk on Queen Anne Avenue North provides a welcome stretch of shade. Oriana follows a few feet behind, carrying *Guilt* in her hand. *Guilt* is a Scottish thriller and mystery series that aired not long ago on BBC2. This is why we stopped by the library, to pick up the DVD. We pass a beauty salon advertising, among other things, "eyelash extension" and "spray tanning". What's spray tanning, I ask Oriana. Do they hose you down with sunlight? It's a fine mist, answers Oriana. They use some kind of chemical. DHA, I think it's called. I forget what it stands for. It's derived from beets and sugar cane. Beauty is a real obsession these days, I snidely declare. I always avert my eyes when I pass one of the many nail salons in the neighborhood. They make me retch. I think it's always been an obsession, Oriana answers. The Greeks were obsessed with beauty. Just look at their sculpture. They believed that a beautiful body was proof of a beautiful mind. If that were true, I interject, Bella Hadid is a genius and Noam Chomsky is a moron. That isn't true of Socrates, Oriana answers; he believed beauty to be untrustworthy, and that it was difficult to define. He distinguishes between the beauty of the body and the beauty of souls, and the beauty of souls is greater in value than the beauty of the body. The soul is nourished by cognitive striving and by contemplating the vast sea of beautiful instances. We continue in silence, mulling this nugget.

This is what philosophy does: it makes everything questionable. Which is why I like it.

Philosophy is a good thing. You don't even have to think philosophically. You just need to feel it. Just a little. It feels good, doesn't it? Philosophy feels good. It distances consciousness, a little, from the wound of existence. It's an attitude. But once you get some arguments going, it heats up. It goes from being a cool summer beverage to a dubious shot of white lightning beneath a full West Virginia moon. Everything comes into question. You come into question. Grass comes into question. Trees and birds and mountains and coal mines (coal mines, definitely) come into question. There are some who use the power of thought to compensate for the feebleness to live. And some who spin it all around until you don't know up from down. We dream of infinity and success but are condemned to the finite and failure. What can you make of that? Besides candles. We never live, we hope to live; and always disposing ourselves to be happy, it is inevitable that we never will be. Said Pascal. But did Pascal ever sip champagne on the shores of ambiguity? Despair and happiness are not mutually exclusive. Melancholy is the happiness of being sad. Said Victor Hugo. And I immediately picture the humpback Charles Laughton holding Maureen O'Hara aloft shouting Sanctuary! Sanctuary! There's nothing wrong with a little diversion. I'm big on diversion. So go. Get up and pour yourself a stiff one. Brace yourself for what follows.

There are 93 penises in the Bayeux Tapestry, 76 trombones in the big parade, around 93 billion trees in the Black Forest of southern Germany, 42 gallons in a barrel of oil, 1,802 miles to the core of the earth, approximately 55 million books in the New York City Public Library and 40 to 300 million sperm per milliliter. But what does all this mean? It means nothing. That's the trouble with quantification: it doesn't reveal the essence of things. It confuses measurement with meaning. It represents an orderly, deterministic universe when the reality is quite different. The reality of our universe is its apparent randomness, its complexity. Complexity is non-deterministic, dynamic sets of relationships with underlying patterns, interconnections, feedback loops, repetition, fractals, rattles, and pterodactyls. This is why I like the simultaneity of mosaics. The mosaic is a music of fragments. I can hear it crackle. The engine of a language bristling with antennae and compound predicates begins to ascend from the sand and bring us on an expedition over mountains and waves. Subject and object. Epistemic modality. Suprasegmental sincerity conditions. Treasuries of antinomian deputation. Ambassadors of fern. Ambassadors of fire. Lobsters playing lacrosse in a lather of expectation. Because when worlds begin to disappear, the thing to do is throw words over them, like nets, and drag them back, to the shore, words flopping in a hysteria of disrupted articulation.

Here's a quick rundown of what's happening. The world is on fire and on the brink of nuclear annihilation. There are devastating heatwaves worldwide, massive wildfires, volcanos erupting, forests dying and rapid glacial melt in Antarctica and Greenland. Jakarta, Indonesia's massive megacity of 30 million people, is sinking due to rapid sea rise. The makers of the Snicker candy bar have apologized to China for saying Taiwan is a country. A 9-foot-long chunk of charred debris resembling an alien obelisk was found wedged vertically upright on a sheep farm in New South Wales, Australia. The debris is most likely a piece from the Dragon capsule that brought four astronauts home from the International Space Station on May 2, 2021. Lebanon has been declared the angriest nation on earth. The five least angry countries were Finland, Mauritius, Estonia, Portugal, the Netherlands. President Leica Fuchs (currently recovering from a heart attack, attributed to an unstable angina) and members of her cabinet have denied that the United States, which has sent more than $180 billion to Ukraine since February, is in recession. A gallon of whole milk sells for $7.40. A gallon of gasoline is nearing the $9 dollar mark. Lake Mead, 17% full, is at its lowest level since the lake first began to fill in 1937 and will most likely be bone dry by the end of summer. Plummeting real estate values and mass migration are soon to follow. The Salton Sea has shrunk 90%, leaving behind oxygen-deprived, highly salinized water with a rotten-egg odor that permeates the surrounding area. All but one species of fish has died off and toxins like arsenic and selenium are carried away on the breeze.

I know. It's hard to take in at once. It takes a while to let it settle into a fine velvety silt of tractable information while the rest of the water turns clear again. Ready for a bit more? Here's a bit more.

It has recently been discovered that macaques conceived during the 2018 California wildfire have worse memories than they previously did and are more passive. Bottlenose dolphins in the northern Egyptian Red Sea rub against mucus-secreting gorgonian coral polyps to self-medicate. The Corn Belt is on track to become unsuitable for corn cultivation by 2100 as the level of aflatoxins in corn is set to rise. The northward movement of the pine beauty moth was fifty years ahead of existing estimates. Fjords are emitting as much methane as the deep ocean. Massive quantities of nanoplastics are distributed in spray and fog. Rainwater everywhere on Earth is unsafe to drink due to "forever chemicals." There may be a mirror universe of particles that interacts with our universe through gravity alone. The Manx shearwater is having difficulty finding fish due to cloudier conditions in the water due to warming temperatures. The source of the Thames has dried up. The Loire in France is on its way to drying up. Likewise the Po, the Rhine, the Danube, the Colorado and Yangtze rivers. Hemocyte counts in lobsters have been reduced. Berkeley's 60-year-old Albatross Pub was forced to close due to the Covid lockdown. The ocean is losing its memory and light-sensing neurons have been revived in the eyes of the dead.

Mattias Desmet, a professor in the department of psycho-analysis and clinical consulting at Ghent University, Belgium, and author of *The Psychology of Totalitarianism*, has theorized that the world is in the grip of mass formation – a dangerous, collective type of hypnosis – as we "bear witness to loneliness, free-floating anxiety, and fear giving way to censorship, loss of privacy, and surrendered freedoms. It is all spurred by a singular, focused crisis narrative that forbids dissident views and relies on destructive groupthink."

The world is not as it should be. I'm not entirely sure what the world should be, but it should not be this. The world should be pierced to the core with its own beauty, amber with amphibian glee, its biodiversity and populations busy translating and working hard to understand one another, closets filled with pretty clothes and hats, courtesies exchanged, symposiums, colloquiums, harmoniums and fleshy protrusions rife with zigzags, U-turns, ambiguities and nuance.

A should-be world requires a conscience, a modicum of reason, a sense of humor, a capacity for nuance, and a good toothbrush. Then everything that should be this or should be that would be this, would be that. Everything, even cats, would be current and actual, completely genuine, palpable as a pedipalp, unimpeachable as a peach dump cake, empirical as a blackberry cobbler with a dollop of vanilla ice cream on top. The world is categorically not a modal auxiliary verb dressed in spandex and honorable intentions. It would be nice to live in a society running on love and decency and altruistic gas. But we don't. Conscience, whatever it may be, the sense of right or wrong or the ability to tell the difference between turpitude and turpentine, or have an inkling as to why killing things for sport and pleasure is a bit odd, is gone, is missing in action, absent, nonexistent, nada, zilch, zero, zip, nihil, naught, diddley-squat, void as the office of an investment firm after a major crash on Wall Street, black as the gleefully malevolent heart of Richard III. This is not a linear world. This is a world of fragments. The spaces in between words. And the words themselves – what are they up to? They do know how to propagate.

It's good to distract the mind. But the mind isn't a bull, and I'm not a matador. I'm a metaphor, dressed in a pink glossolalia with tender buttons and a delinquent hat. The more the universe unravels the more it disappears until it doesn't exist at all and then pops into life like a full-blown satori. Whenever I'm in a quandary, I start opening fortune cookies. A real distress is better than a fake joy. The requirement of lucidity takes precedence over the desire to be happy. Of course, if I'm not up to being lucid, that's cool. Obscurity has its rewards. And confusion doesn't know the difference. The truth is often bitter. But coffee lovers know what pleasure there is in a little bitterness. Sugar destroys it. I trust salt. I don't trust sugar, even though I love sugar. I know the truth of sugar. Sugar is sophistry. Salt is method. The beautiful is what despairs.

Oriana, my wife of 28 years, is reading in the other room. She's also been watching tutorials on YouTube about the care of orchids. This is the third month of her retirement. It's been a time of renaissance and leisure for the two of us. Were it not for all the scary developments elsewhere in the world, we'd be cultivating the serenity required for the inevitable abrasions of age. She's better at keeping the world at bay than I am. I tend to rant and wave my arms about and channel my inner Hicks. She doesn't like it much when I do this in public. I get carried away. I get loud and begin flailing or bow my head and stare fixedly at an imaginary device while I walk, mimicking the lifeless shuffle of the brain-dead phone zombies, knuckleheads paying more attention to their phones than their dogs or toddlers. Even even-tempered Oriana has cause to wonder. Why do they have dogs? Why do they have kids? All they need is a phone. But what is it, what is so enthralling that they can't take their eyes away even when they're outside presumably for a walk with their dog or pushing a perambulator? Is it the news? Are they, like me, expecting a world-annihilating flash at any minute? Crop failure and famine? Another celebrity entering rehab?

Oriana thinks it has something to do with dopamine. Getting "likes" and comments on social media. A recent report states: "Screen use releases dopamine in the brain, which can negatively affect impulse control ... studies have shown screen time affects the frontal cortex of the brain, similar to the effect of cocaine. Similar to drugs, screen time sets off a pleasure/reward cycle that can have a negative impact on your life."

I've had cocaine. I don't see the similarity. "Cocaine," poet Michael McClure observed, "is an ace of sunlight. The darkness in skull and gut lights up ... As the high comes, there is a flurry of excitement and speaking and laughter; eyes are bright and clear. It is erotically stimulating. There is friendliness and creativity." The sad, preoccupied faces I see bent down to their screens do not appear to have sunlight racing through their brains, or friendliness and creativity. Though I could be wrong. I can't really make those calls. Still. There is what I see, and what I see is deadness, numbness, and deep self-absorption. Lusterless eyes. Or the tourists getting off of those sight-seeing tours, sleepy-eyed, stepping onto a crowded sidewalk as if in a trance.

It happened. I swore it wasn't going to happen, not to me, but it happened. I became one of those guys, those old farts shaking and nodding their heads sagely, "... back in my day."

I'm old enough to know better but I'm still young enough to confuse the entire issue. I'm best when I'm at my worst. And every time I complete a circle around the sun I make a chalk mark on the ceiling. I now have a ceiling full of chalk marks. Which makes me feel a little like chalk. It looks like someone turned Switzerland upside down. I've never seen so many clocks. So many little gears. And why should that make me feel like chalk? Maybe it's my tie. It's off-white. And off-kilter. And not really a tie at all. It's a symptom for a disease that hasn't been invented yet. I'm working on it. I have various oddities on the shelf, some of which pump chimeras out of the ground like Texas pumpjacks. This is my way of drilling the unconscious. If you stop by on Thursday I'll give you a sample of scraggly and a jar of sound. I put words out like traps. I want to catch an idea at the moment it's happening. They gestate like mollusks, then sneak up on a brain and scare the shit out of it. And that's what we call writing. It's why no one reads; it's too frightening, and full of ideas that rattle your cage and keep you from sleep.

I'm often accused of being judgmental. Which is silly. Of course I'm judgmental. Who isn't judgmental? Isn't calling someone judgmental judgmental? I dare anyone to go ten minutes without using their judgment. If they can go an entire ten minutes without injury or death, I'll be quite willing to congratulate them, admit my error, and give myself pause before I judge in the future. But I won't stop judging because it feels too damn good to be wrong.

Hear that? That would be the neighbor upstairs making breakfast, ostensibly, though it sounds more like he's building an airplane.

Above my desk, a group of hunters return with a pack of dogs. It would appear, since they're not carrying any deer or wild boar, that the hunt was not successful. There's snow on the ground and two people maintain a fire in front of a house. In the distance, at the bottom of a large hill, people ice skate. It's a print of a 1565 oil-on-wood painting by Pieter Bruegel the Elder. I've had it many years and have always been fond of it. I find the silent acceptance of the hunters deeply moving, their silence. Each of them seems deep in thought.

How strange to have lived so long I've got a past with a real history. A past that could be in a textbook, in which people wonder how we managed to endure this world. This air. This era. This burp in time. Look back, look back my children, look at those naked people jumping into a lake. Look at those colors. Look at those smiles. Look at those helicopters passing over, so black, so mysterious, and so loud. What was it like to walk around without a phone? The phones were left behind. They were usually attached to a wall, and surrounding the phone was a galaxy of numbers jotted down in pen or pencil. They were left at home to ring when nobody was there to answer. And if you were home, well, you had to answer. This connected people. You couldn't "screen" calls. It was harder to isolate yourself. You knew where you stood.

"Ghosting" is a strange new phenomenon. People have gotten good at canceling, effacing, rendering one another null and void. You can become a pariah in a split second; all it takes is one faux pas, one careless remark, and you're dead. Gone. X, Y or Z cease responding to your calls and emails.

Being a ghost has its advantages. It's nice not having to be "on" all the time. There's a sweetness to anonymity. Sartre famously said "Hell is other people." Being a pariah is not among the worst things that can happen to you.

Up until the '60s, nobody paid much attention to you. Not until you grew your hair out and looked like one of those English rockers, Keith Richards or Mick Jagger: the bad boys. If you were a guy, being bad meant a lot of things, most of them erroneous; but not always. Wildness and disregard come in a thousand different flavors, including impulse, spontaneity, debauchery, immoderation, and snake. Bad was good then. Even the girls got in on the game and got a little sassy, a little devil-may-care. Most often being cool just meant standing aside to let the world happen. It was a game of control. As long as nobody tried to control you, you were cool. There was a large appetite for excitement, the new, the way-out, the inventive, the daring. That world is so completely gone now it tastes like history, with a pinch of stress and a spoonful of saudade.

I do have theories for things, but I don't want to get into that. I want to have some fun here. Let's not get into isms, or prisons, or apanage, or coroner's reports. I'm happy to be here, that's all. Hammering words. Building belvederes. Disassembling indignities. Mapping a future.

Sometimes a stain will seem to be a spider, and when you lean down to get a closer look it's a blur without detail, and so, yes, a stain, not a creature with eight thin legs reposing on the carpet, or dead, with its legs curled into a ball. Facts can be like that, too. They'll appear to be one thing but when you look more closely you can see that the mark is either a spider or a stain, and if a spider, what kind of spider, and if a stain, what kind of stain. Or like a dark spot on the root of an orchid that turns out to be a form of fungus. A vein, or a particle of gold in a pan of sand. I feel like one of those old guys who's lived a long and varied life and feels obligated to dispense advice. But the fact remains that there's a whole lot of stuff that whizzed past my head when I was in my 20s that I stop to take a good hard look at now. And if there's one thing I did know in my 20s that turned out to be far truer than imagined it's that everything is interrelated. It seems trivial because it has been said so many times, but pondered more generously, proves to be stunning in its veracity. Vehemently, vertiginously, voluminously true. Interrelated as the symbiotic network between fungi and plant roots, which is so essential it has a name: mycorrhiza.

I don't live in a forest of signs. I live in a forest of daffodils. A dale of diversions. A clutter of aims that were never achieved. A trickle of meaning on a wall of slime. A helter-skelter existence of red feathers and seething passions. An amber ambivalence in a violet mood. A war of nerves. A proximity to silk. A slammed door. An open heart. A fastened belt and a loosened tie. A sow with a sore and a cow with a riddle. A photograph of Roger Waters. "Heartbreak Hotel." An acre of ocher and a scholar of goats. That's where I live. That house over there. Made of throats.

There's a spot where I like to pause. It's at the halfway mark of a run Oriana and I do in the afternoon, a small space off the pedestrian walkway shaded by two European hornbeams. It was especially nice today. The high was in the lower 80s. This is the spot where we turn around and run back the way we came. It's interesting to me, the way the exact route I traveled looks completely different when I reverse direction. Is perception that easily tricked, fooled, renewed? Apparently so. It's a benefit. Like getting a coupon for a free Milky Way, or a Great Clips haircut. Which makes me wonder if this same principle might apply to anything unfortunate, the so-called silver lining. Is it true, or just another vapid bromide? Is there a silver lining to abrupt climate change? It does enhance appreciation of the planet we're on. I don't understand Elon Musk's preoccupation with Mars. Unless he has a more acute understanding of the predicament we're in and settling on Mars appears to be the best alternative. There is definitely an allure to the Martian landscape, though I don't understand it, don't understand the allure. It's just rock and sky. Wherever you look, rock and sky. Not a blue sky. A pink sky. Maybe that's it. The harsh red desolation complemented by a vast pink sky in which the sun hangs a tad smaller than it appears on planet Earth. Is that what a silver lining looks like? Maybe it would if I were there. But from here it's just a dream, a fantasy, and fantasies are fine by themselves, they don't require silver linings, only a modicum of truth and some nice upholstery. The atmosphere on Mars is thin and non-respirable for human lungs. But there's a silver lining there: if you're cooking up your own atmosphere, you can add a little extra oxygen, maybe goose it a little with some nitrous oxide, and voila! Silver lining. If I were to become the mogul of a cruise line I'd call it the Silver Lining Cruise Line and visit all the ports of the equatorial regions where the sunsets are profligate displays of unscrupulous beauty, variegated hues of savage delicacy. The kind of place where anguish goes to die and become reincarnated as a dolphin.

Once, when I was a young man of one and twenty, I learned to play "Beautiful Dreamer" by Stephen Foster on a flute, and became instantly transported out of a North Dakota farm into an alpine meadow somewhere near Geneva, where the wildflowers and craggy summits attracted poets like Percy Bysshe Shelley and Lord Byron, and where Mary Shelley, giddy with the thunder and lightning of a summer storm, created a solitary monster whose silver linings are the fall of some vast fragment, the thunder sound of the avalanche, or the cracking reverberated along the mountains of the accumulated ice.

It's 5.45 p.m., summer, the modern era, and I'm old. Soon to be 75. Mortality acquires a very sharp flavor at this age. Tart, pungent, vinegary. Not crisp like an apple, but soft like a peach, and messy. Juice dribbling from the mouth. Thoughts dripping in the mind like calcium carbonate, forming stalactites and stalagmites, chambers full of bones, extraordinary formations, limestone galleries haunted with the jukebox glow of reflection. "The world is a bad place" sang the late Dean Jones of Marmalade, "a terrible place to live. Oh, but I don't want to die."

No hope without fear, said Spinoza. Our brightest hopes are when we're scared to death. So yes. I'm full of hope. Stuffed to the gills with it. Bubbling over with hopium. I know what I see on a billboard is a lie, but I can't take my eyes off it. Life never corresponds to our hopes. But it doesn't mean our lives went off the tracks. It doesn't mean we got cheated. Life does what it can. What it does best. Which is live. Breathe in. Breathe out.

The story continues. It always does. With you or without you. It keeps going. Your story. My story. The story of Frankenstein. The story of sutures. The story of creation. The story of X. The story of O. The story of shopping for pomegranates and buying a pair of socks instead. The universe craves sequence. Expansion. Elaboration. Morning to night, it's never the story we expected. It's the one that ate our plans and coughed up a fuchsia in the middle of a chess game with a skeletal being named Gangrene. The plot is a structural presupposition which progresses according to plan. This is why stories are so comforting. Any progression is comforting. Regression is a sad bowl of soup in a run-down café in lower Manhattan in the '40s. But that's not what this is. This is breaking ice. This is taking an ax to chop up the frozen sea inside us, to paraphrase Kafka. There's no horizon, no street signs, no map. Just a hill. And a rock.

A man sat down in a paragraph but the paragraph didn't exist yet. There was a table and a chair in a room of tables and chairs, and so the paragraph grew, and as the paragraph grew the man's thoughts about birth began their own odyssey of ontogeny, and the man wondered why he couldn't remember being born. It was as traumatic as anything else – dying, or war, or a car accident – so why couldn't he remember that moment of floating in amniotic bliss, when suddenly there were spasmodic movements and he was ejected from bliss and slid through a membranous canal and a pair of forceps clamped on his head and pulled him into the world. Funny how people don't remember this, though maybe in some unconscious way they do. Perhaps it's an underlying anxiety that everyone tries to overcome and some do and some don't and those that do mature into calm and reasonable people whereas those who don't become chronically anxious and distrustful. And as these thoughts circulated in his mind, the paragraph continued to grow, and he had the acute sense that someone must be writing it, and who was this person, and would it happen again, would he be sitting at a table enjoying a cup of coffee and suddenly be ejected and sent sliding into another dimension? Or were these his words forming the paragraph, his consciousness causing this structure to grow and become a skein of words unraveling various aspects of existence? And this was how energy became mass and the universe itself came into being; a primordial chaos of quarks and electrons aggregating to form protons and neutrons which combined into nuclei, and as the universe cooled and continued to expand, electrons trapped around nuclei formed the first atoms, which formed helium and hydrogen and carbon and oxygen and iron and the hearts of stars, spectacular stellar explosions, and heat and light, and a supposed entity called dark matter holding it all together. Dark matter is indiscernible. It can't be observed. Its existence is speculative. Its presence is implied by the gravitational effects coalescing around the agglomeration of words in a small room with a few tables and chairs. A bit of music. Some coffee. And a man sitting down.

When one paragraph ends, another begins. It has to. Nothing can remain static for long. Like the man said, what does not change is the will to change. Don't rush it. One can only absorb so much. Too much information drowns awareness in an unavailing extravaganza. It's more convenient to become aware of this interrupted change, this subtle disruption in the field of energy, and to notice it only when it becomes large enough to impress on the body a new attitude, and feed the attention a new direction. Take things in stride. Drink it in slowly. Don't gulp. Doing nothing is doing anything. And doing anything is doing everything.

For example, I can't predict with total accuracy what's going to happen within the next few hours. The other night, when president pro tem Flora Ferrari flew to Taiwan to thumb her nose at China, I thought it would be our last. An annihilating flash would occur during the night and we'd be so instantly and painlessly obliterated we wouldn't even know it had happened. This has been, in fact, for the past few years, a daily reality. People have lost their frigging minds. It has become a stale truism to say the times are uncertain, or the times are interesting. The current zeitgeist is one of raving lunacy. It's a monster that, after eons of dissatisfaction and accumulations of wealth that have depleted what the planet is able to supply, has realized, perhaps unconsciously, that the inability to find gratification is a curse, but rather than seek ways to remove the curse, don the robes of a Zen monk à la Thich Nhat Hanh and go walking down a path in the Dordogne smiling at the world's creatures, they buy more yachts, build more missiles, drop more bombs, unhouse and displace more people, and erect higher walls to keep the immigrants at bay.

So why worry? Good question. I've been trying to answer that my entire life. We all know the ultimate outcome of our own personal lives, these smaller narratives that weave in and out of the bigger one. It ends. Even if one is reborn, reincarnated as a bird or cockroach, king or queen, or an industrial maven with a bank account bigger than Luxembourg, it's really not you, it might be a shade of you, but it's not you, maybe the energy of you, but that energy is the same energy of all souls. The you with a name and a habitat and a curriculum vitae, is gone. Forever gone. Most of us are as aware of this as the names of our children or the make of our car or the price of gasoline. But some impish little gremlin in us keeps the flame alive, the notion that not knowing the date of our demise is an indication, however absurdly irrational, that it might go on forever.

This is why a vision of linearity is such a false vision. The universe is multi-dimensional. There may well be more than one universe. There's no real beginning or middle or end to anything. It's all a mosaic. A multi-dimensional mosaic. An entire museum of mosaics, with a few sculptures thrown in. A Joseph Beuys here, a Louise Bourgeois over there. A rattling-rackling-spitting-crashing Métamatic by Jean Tinguely has run off with the museum director, a pretty angel named Dubraska Nebraska. And that spidery little creature in the corner who claims to be God is molding a new planet, all eight legs working frantically while the pedipalps attend to every little detail. And now, if you'll excuse me, I must absent myself a while to go check whether the upstairs neighbor is finished with his wash so I can run a load in the washer.

Was Ludwig Wittgenstein a clean man? I bet he was. His writing certainly is: clean as a chess move, queen's bishop to g5. Lean, clean, and deeply puzzling.

What Wittgenstein called the "true enough" isn't quite true enough. It needs to be a little more aesthetic, ornamented with bells and rubies and big muscular arms, so that we can move this cave around in segments, finding bits of bone in the dust, words brawling around a torch on the wall like Paleolithic shadows, horses and bison and shamanistic bears as our body heat warms the apartment. Marc Chagall depicted himself with flowers at the age of 97. You may depict yourself any way you want, but if you dip your brush in dispensation, the bourbon will feel better when it enters the bloodstream and you can feel your heart beating a few short miles from the ocean.

Oriana and I go to Discovery Park for a short walk. Oriana – newly retired, as I said earlier – is radiant, reflective, and irreproachable. Discovery Park is a large, 534-acre park densely populated with conifers, red alders and bigleaf maples. We wanted to hear birds. Oriana has an app on her phone that picks up the sound of a bird and then tells you its name. We had to walk into the forest a small distance to get away from the noises of the city – weed trimmers, lawn mowers, trucks, jets, leaf blowers, etc. – to find an adequate amount of quiet to hear some birds. We headed up a narrow dirt path and her phone began immediately picking up birds, none of which I could hear thanks to my tinnitus. These included dark-eyed junco, Hutton's Vireo, white-crowned sparrow, barn swallow, northern flicker, song sparrow, American crow, golden-crowned kinglet, cedar waxwing, chestnut-backed chickadee, Pacific-slope fly-catcher, spotted towhee, purple finch, and house finch.

We took a scenic route and gazed out over the sound to Bainbridge Island. Nearby were some large houses with columned porches, which had once been the officer's quarters when Fort Lawton was still in operation. What a remarkable place to live.

We approached a meadow of long grasses constellated with bright yellow dandelions and hundreds of swallows darting about. It's spellbinding to watch them in flight. They fly with great creativity and perform aerial maneuvers with mercurial agility. A colorful parasail emerged over the ridge and I went down to see what was going on. There was no sign of a parasailer when I got down there. I found this puzzling. We walked a few yards to the north and discovered a man arranging his parasail for another try. There was barely any wind. The man got his sail ready and began running down the hill. He was able to lift his legs a little, but not for long. The paraglider chute is essentially a wing, and like all wings, it's curved to quicken the flow of air over the top surface, thereby reducing the pressure *above* the wing while simultaneously increasing the pressure *below* the wing. This differential in airspeed is what creates lift, and the breeze was just too weak to make that happen for the paraglider. He gave it another try, then gave up, folded his chute, packed it into a large blue bag and left. Disappointing. I really wanted to see him fly.

Later, at home, I was curious to see what kind of bird I might be. I whistled and Oriana held her phone, with the app on, at me. I was quickly identified as a purple-crested nincompoop.

I have a longing for a world that is gone. The world where we had a choice of movies and movie theaters, and places to eat, fun places, cheap places and expensive places, funky places and elegant places, funky places in fancy places and fancy places in funky places. Affordable apartments. Affordable houses. And, most importantly, the secure knowledge that there would be food on the shelves in all the grocery stores. That the world was humming along fine and had a future. Maybe not the big bright pretty future we all anticipated, but a future where the mail was still delivered, cars sold and repaired, the garbage picked up, the parks maintained, and abundant stores with an infinite miscellany of goods and services to choose from. A time when you didn't need a mask, a medical document to be permitted to participate in society, a huge income for basic housing, or the anxiety of always having to police your speech and behavior. Any way we can get that world back? What would it take? A moving van? Please tell me, I've got to know. Include water. Lots of water. That went missing fast. Everything went with it: the Bill of Rights, good books with good bookstores to sell them, and coin-operated parking meters.

Is going to the moon now become so banal the billionaires are doing it? What happened to so disenchant people that video games and social media clicks will take precedence over the profusion of feeling and sensation pressing against the nerves with gentle urgency each minute of the day? Or am I being presumptuous? Bad habit, presumption; I will presume no more. Nor will I assume. I will what? What I don't know. Bowl? I will bowl. I will brandish a sword. I will box my shadow. And what shall I do if my shadow wins? I will accommodate the world as best I can, and cast a long shadow. There's nothing banal about the dark. Darkness is always interesting. You can find the strangest things in the dark, things that are otherwise hidden by daylight. You can find yourself in the dark. You will find that you're a ghost haunting your own life. You will find parallels with cow bells and groundswells with nerve cells. Learn to throw a knife. Stumble into Tucson drunk as a skunk and pick a fight with the person you were three minutes ago. But yes, it's true, billionaires are going to the moon. Billionaires like going everywhere. Except inside. Was it a bright afternoon, asks the literary type sitting in a chair. He looks like Rod Serling. In fact, it is Rod Serling. He's been sitting in the dark. He's looking for new material. Did you find it, Rod? He found there is more to the twilight zone than either a zone or a twilight. This is what comes of living in a time of billionaires. All the natural laws are bent and contorted into pretzels of salty logic. Very little makes sense anymore. Conversations lead to contusions. Best to sit back and let things happen on their own. Let it go. Sail by intuition. The fragrances in the air.

Ever have days when everything feels like a fight? I can't even rip off a panel of paper towel lately without a struggle. Just as we cannot think of spatial objects at all apart from space, or temporal objects apart from time, so we cannot think of any object apart from the possibility of its connections with other things, particularly perforated things, things like paper towels and voting ballots, office forms, questionnaires, surveys, invoices and stamps, and this goes by the name of tedium, which is rumored to be a fundamental fact of existence, as are boating and mounting museum exhibitions and seeking employment. There are other things to consider as well, nascent forms of drool that occasion a napkin, a moment of discretion, before it gets out of control, and the witches in *Macbeth* may be heard laughing in the background.

Human biology is awkward. A typical day is spent sneezing, pissing, shitting and finding the appropriate venue for performing these biological functions in private. This is the private theater of the self, Möbius loops of inner dialogue troubling and dilating our existence with its electrochemical rhetoric, singing elixirs radically transforming our perceptions, fueling our grievances with intercessory hilarities of fiction. Here, for example, is Act I: the curtain rises on a married couple arguing about a kitchen remodeling job. Their words rush hot from bright chrome faucets, registering a new era in human relations, a renaissance of manners in which the quirkiness of human existence will find a bold new Shaw to show us the phantoms of our neuroses and the follies of our choices. I must arise and go now, to blow my nose.

But this is not my ambition. I have no ambition. This is one of the great advantages of getting old: no future, no goal. Nothing to attain, nothing to reach. Just sitting and breathing. And eating, of course. Eating is wonderful. I recently heard John Cleese remark on how wonderful food becomes when one becomes old. I could see the results of that in the magnificent paunch protruding from his otherwise stately and well-proportioned physique.

Freedom is what we do with what is done to us. Said Sartre. We are our choices.

Here are some choices I made today. I chose to close the door to our bedroom rather than continue to be pestered by our cat, who is very sweet but eats too much, it's all she wants to do. I've tried playing with her, and reading passages from Dante's *Divine Comedy*, all to no avail. I feel her claws penetrate the skin of my knee through the fabric of my pants, and realize what a strange world we live in, that we should adopt other species with which to form an affectionate bond, and then proceed to embroil ourselves in a tug-of-war between appetite and prudence.

I chose to go for a run around the crown of Queen Anne Hill and feed the many crows there. Perhaps I should use the present tense, choose, since it is a choice I make every day, with gladness and enthusiasm. It is my LSD: Long Slow Distance running.

Oriana chose – chooses – to come with me, as she often does, and feeds blue jays as well as crows, with whom she has made a casual bond of mutual trust and communion.

I chose to get up at 8.00 a.m., which is a good hour to rise, and clamber out of bed.

I chose to eat scrambled eggs and yogurt, to which I added a big glop of cherry jelly and a sprinkling of blueberries.

Fifty-four years ago I made a choice not to participate in war, but since it was not an allowable choice at the time, there being an imperative set by the government, a compulsory recruitment called a draft – a completely unsuitable word for a draconian, state-mandated enlistment into violence and terror – it was a choice that required some strategy and sacrifice to bring to fruition.

I chose catalysis over catalpa in a sentence I wrote earlier today in a letter I wrote to the International Catfish Society concerning the Brobdingnagian barbels of the Babylonian Bullhead. This created a pandemonium among all the other words, but was worth it in the end. "Every thing is, as it were, in a space of possible atomic facts," remarked Ludwig Wittgenstein. "I can think of space as empty, but not of the thing without space." Or catalysis, or catfish. Sooner or later there will be a need for catalpa. I will make sure of it. I shall choose to employ it.

I chose to purchase many books and create a library of sizable proportion, lugging boxes upon boxes whenever I moved, many of which remain in storage to this day, awaiting delivery from bondage and to be rediscovered.

I chose to frolic and freely indulge in the Dionysian mysteries of alcohol, and then – finding this path somewhat arduous – the road of excess leading, eventually, to the palace of wisdom, I discontinued this practice, though without abandoning excess entirely, as excess bobbles on the dashboard of adventure, bold and golden as morning.

I chose to learn French, which is the domain of Charles Baudelaire, Stephane Mallarmé, Guillaume Apollinaire and Arthur Rimbaud.

I chose to continue my exploration of consciousness, which is as strange a phenomenon as anything else discovered so far within the bounds of this universe, but for which there has not yet been discovered a valid explanation as to its dynamics or causes, or where or why self-awareness comes into play and finds its purport enameled by persuasive argument, its vaporous speculations pinched and squeezed from the air, and its essence distilled into jugs of white lightning in the woods and hills of West Virginia where the rabbits are swift and the owl is king.

Those of us who ponder such weighty and ultimately foolish pursuits – given the ponderous nature of time and its grave limitations and the need for shelter and food – have done so of our own free will, by choice and predilection, and secreted ourselves from the public eye in order to liberate ourselves from the bias and pressure of expectation, of playing to the audience, and where it is considered strange to indulge such whims, season our pilaf with peppery jouissance.

Someone hands me a menu of options by which to die and I choose the filet of thunder, with a side dish of lava and sand heated into glass, the special of the day, which is an Icelandic volcano erupting, and a bowl of universe expanding against the membranes of space and time. I can feel my nerves propel me through the vague waves of a pulsar. I get up from the table and decide to go elsewhere. Death suddenly doesn't seem very appealing. I'll come back later, when I'm more in the mood. But a skeleton at the door takes me by the arm and sits me down at the table again. This is the good and greasy Nobody Gets Out Alive Café and I came in here for a juicy hamburger and a bag of fries and a lemonade. Yes, lemonade. I've just discovered it. I didn't like it as a kid. Too tart. I was obsessed with sugar. And we know where that leads. It leads to warm embraces and big wet kisses. Nobody wants to die. What are we doing here? This isn't the right place. Not the right place at all. Gimme shelter. Gimme doughnuts. But mostly give me time and I'll get this figured out. The whole shebang. The entire shit show. And then get a milkshake.

I read a piece from *The Art of the Sonnet* by Ted Berrigan which ends with an invitation to call him, and a phone number. So I give him a call. Ted answers and says "Hello." I say "Hi, is this Ted?" "Yes. Who were you expecting? Shelley?" "No, no, you, I was hoping to hear your voice. It sounds just like I thought it would, a bit rough." I hear Ted clear his throat and cough a little. "Sorry," he says. "I haven't had occasion to use my throat for about 39 years." "What's it like being dead?" "Hard to say," he answered. "There are no words for it. Words belong in your dimension. Up here we just sing. Gospel, mostly. And the bowling alleys stay open all night. There's bingo and badminton. And ping pong. I played ping pong with Dennis Hopper yesterday." "Who won?" "Dennis. What you think?" "What about harps and angels?" "Art and angles?" "No, harps and angels." "The art is what you make of it. The heaven is in the doing of it. There are angles to that. It's all in the angles, son. Birds to be looked at, pills, a warm bath. Winds in the stratosphere. The moon is yellow. My nose is red. Death is a lovely place. Say hi to the malcontents downstairs." "I will. Meanwhile, I must thank you, Ted. This has been most informative." "No problem. I was hoping someone might call. So hey, thank you! Thanks for calling. And for reading my poem." "The pleasure was entirely mine." Click, and goodbye.

I've been a weirdo my whole life. It's why I gravitate toward people who look like they've been leading a peculiar life in the desert. Captain Beefheart, for example. Remember him? He lived in the desert and looked like someone who lived in the desert. He painted wildly abstract pictures and devoted a song to crows, "Ice Cream for Crow." He made a video to go with it, but it was too weird for MTV, so it didn't get aired. I discovered it on YouTube a few years ago. I was charmed by it.

The song begins with Beefheart (whose real name was Don Vliet – the Van an affectation) silhouetted against an orange desert sky with a blazing sun just above a tower of high-tension power lines and a few Saguaro cactuses. Beefheart wears a floppy fedora and is accompanied by the four members of The Magic Band, a drummer and three guitarists, all jumping up and down and squirming and bending over as if in thrall to some powerful spirit of music they've awakened and can barely contain. Beefheart declaims the lyrics as if it were a speech ("It's so hot / looks like you have three beaks crow / the moon is so full / white hat on a pumpkin"), while making broad gestures and telegramming expressions of portentous zeal. The song has a goofy rhythm and an even goofier melody. The notes sound flexed and stretched and bent, attuned to another dimension. The scene switches from day to night to day again rendering time and space elastic and volatile. A few of Beefheart's paintings, inserted into the video and held up for display, help define the complete zaniness of the moment.

I never got to meet Mr Van Vliet, who passed away in December 2010. I wish I could have. I feel we'd have had a lot in common. I love art, I love deserts, and I love crows and ice cream. I love anything strange and eccentric. I put the paintings of Van Gogh high on my list of things to love, and Gerard de Nerval and Edgar Allan Poe. Misfits with a taste for the bizarre, the macabre. For refined narcotics and voluptuous pleasures in Gothic castles under gray skies and a raucous chorus of crows. What a colossal ego, yes. Hard work. Egos require a lot of care and attention. A big theatre and the consequences that go with it. Splintered doors, broken bottles, a knife through the heart. Go with anything romantic and you're bound to bump into big, overblown Byronic gestures. That said, you don't want to take it too seriously, either. Allow for incongruities. Laughable contradictions. Mystics in Cadillacs. The New York art world. Ice cream for crows.

What I'm describing is the aristocrat of the soul that Poe believed was the lot of the artist. I believe artists are born this way. Art is not a rational vocation. No rational individual would willfully choose to put their inner demons on display as a form of career. This is where sublimation comes in. The most bizarre impulses can be made to shine in a Beethoven sonata. The darkest thought can be made to glitter like a jewel if the artist is equal to the labor required. Sometimes there are compensations for this in the form of money. But commodity and art are generally strangers to one another. Most often it's a glorious way to fill a solitude and bring before our senses everything that a spirit can perceive or conceive. Stand back, grimace, and start again.

When the obstetrician clamped those forceps around my soft baby skull and pulled me into this world, I wasn't quite ready for it. For any of it. Facial expressions. Handshakes. Loud noises. For life, for love, for the world at large. For backyard barbecues, the stories of Boxcar Willy, or final results of a quart of tequila. No baby is. That's what makes them babies. But I'm a fully fledged septuagenarian now, been around the block a few times, and I'm still ill-equipped to deal with the vagaries and psychopathy of human society in the 21st century. What have I learned in all my years here? Good question. I still have trouble with clamshell packaging. For the time being, I just want to say how good it feels to be here, welding words together in a cloud of sparks and bluish smoke, building a chassis for the combustive pistons of the written word.

Poverty is bound to enter the picture sooner or later, so let's talk about it. I'll just come out and say it: poverty sucks. It has the potential to create friction among friends, and even if things get ironed out, can you honestly say it enriched the friendship? Maybe it did. If so, here's a sly wink at poverty. But don't get too chummy.

Poverty really does a number on family relations. Not everybody is graced with a brother like Theo Van Gogh. If one chooses a career trajectory that puts one's financial security

at risk, legitimate imputations of selfishness and self-indul-
gence will taint one's closest relations. We live in a world
where technology has greatly expanded our ability to
achieve certain goals but its tendency toward authoritarian-
ism and manipulation and coercion of needs has also
resulted in a narrowing of perspective and an acute sense of
alienation. The dominance of anti-democratic monopolistic
corporations has resulted in a cruel and crude dystopia for
those excluded from its rewards. Things now are just down-
right neo-feudal. Meaning futile. That's when you turn to
Eshu, trickster god of the Yoruba. And rants and insults and
the balm of solitude.

If you listen to music on your headphones long enough it
becomes a cloud chamber. Bands from the distant past step
out of the fog. Steppenwolf, Soft Machine, Moby Grape,
Foghat. That's quite a show you've got going on the top of
your head, says a stranger at the bus stop holding a jar with
something dark in it. I've seen all those bands. Want to see
my tarantula? Sure, I say, and out it comes. I don't know
what to say. I don't want to hurt this person's feelings, but
this is not a tarantula. It's a nipple from a baby bottle. Don't
worry, it won't bite, he says. He's cute, I say. He doesn't say
anything. I don't think he wanted to hear that his tarantula
was cute. Pretending things are one way rather than
another is a sticky entanglement of perspectives and beliefs.
You have to exercise a little caution. Sometimes words will
gather a certain energy, jump the fence and run off to create
their own universe. So be it. In dropping all false concep-
tions, I dropped the one true thing in the entire bunch and
it shattered into a thousand glittering lies. I picked the pret-
tiest one and put it on my head. And Lightnin' Hopkins
walked out of the mist.

If asked to choose an anthem expressive of the current zeitgeist, I would choose "Gimme Shelter" by The Rolling

Stones. Those opening notes of "Gimme Shelter" are brilliant. They build suspense then release an emotional state of crisis: "Oh, a storm is threatening / My very life today / If I don't get some shelter / Oh yeah I'm gonna fade away." Many of us (you know who they are) feel under siege. Those lyrics were born during the tumultuous sixties but are no less appropriate for the stresses of the current age. The corporate juggernaut is crushing everything we hold near and dear. The freedom to say what you want without having your life canceled. The freedom to roam, hitch a ride, blindfold yourself and throw a dart at a map and wherever it lands will be your next destination. Go live in a town you've never been and lead a life in which work and leisure are nicely and sanely balanced and there is time to visit museums, skip stones on the languid rivers of the valley, resolve tensions and unravel the great mysteries of life with books on art and poetry stacked high on a kitchen table alongside a bottle of wine.

You could live like Kerouac and Cassady up until the '90s and then it got impossible. So that's part of it, part of the problem, and the continuing nightmare of "Gimme Shelter," which is now literal, as many are without shelter. Homeless encampments all across the country in vacant lots, railroad sidings and rundown city parks. It seems like a warning. As is Julian Assange.

"Gimme Shelter" means shelter from the erosion of free speech, plagues, pandemics, mass shootings, militarized police. Because most of us feel the same. Same angst. Same set of assumptions. Expectations. Mindset. Ideas about morality and behavior. How to build highways and raise geraniums. There's still that, still a little magnetism there. It's the topography that has changed. The way we commune, or don't. Because, you know, Covid and all that shit. Remember buskers? Rob Falsini busking at Covent Gardens, singing "Chasing Cars" by Snow Patrol. People shopping, pausing to listen. That was just a few years ago. And already it feels like a lost and distant time, a time never to come again. Lost as the old gold and silver mines in the Rockies, deep dark holes in the mountain, old splintered lumber blocking the entrance.

Alas, the seas hath cast me on the rocks, washed me from shore to shore, and left my breath nothing to think on but ensuing death. Said Pericles, to no one in particular. He was alone. But words of a similar brand and character do inhabit my outlook. My trajectory. My weltschmerz. Especially in the morning when I get out of bed. When I first put my feet on the floor and stand erect. I feel like an astronaut who has just landed on a fabulous but highly enigmatic planet.

You know the feeling: you must re-enter the world. Wash your face, brush your teeth, brush your hair. Prepare to acclimatize. Adapt. Adjust. Tuck your shirt in. Pull your socks up. The day must be approached with caution, with a little circumspection and a reservoir of lived experience.

I defy fashion. I wear what I want. Today I'm wearing thin. My buttons are tender and my pants feel like an after-thought rubbing against my legs. Not hard. Soft. Like thought. Only my collar is alert to other possibilities. It's upright, like Elvis's jewel-encrusted collar. I sparkle all over with reconciliation. The instant I put two words together in an artful fashion I was doomed to a life of social marginality. But I wanted to look good, you know. Even if it's just a trip from the living room to the kitchen, I want to confront the whole idea of fashion with a sandwich in my hand. Most people think automatically of rainbow trout. Not me. Provolone on rye. Dear Life: thank you for all the bitterness and ice cream. Conformity is the easiest solution. But it's as evil as a QR code. You want to look dangerous. Be that person standing outside looking in. Hungry. And a little bit crazy.

It's why I turned to philosophy. The well is deep and compelling, the water so cold it stuns the mind. But it's not absolutes that make the water so cold and thrilling, it's the transiency, the flux of temperature and mood. It's those fleeting moments of perceived truth, for lack of a better word, that prove invaluable. They transcend value altogether. And they're extremely hard to catch. It's all in the flow, the current, the trill of birds, the rustle of wind in the trees, the allure of the sublime. And what is the sublime? We know what it is when we see it, but what is it?

Whatever it is, it resists the constrictions of language. That's what makes it sublime. It's the exquisite danger of the ineffable, the precariousness of its ice. The nearness of death in the risk of its proximity. Language is impoverished by the intensity of these things, the raw immediacy of the cosmos in the guise of a rock, a wall of granite by which your body hangs from a pinch.

This is where meaning comes in. Meaning protects us from the immediate by giving us an actuary for the actual. I spend my entire day doing this. Making meaning. Constructing meaning. Assembling meaning. Putting meaning in stories that shuffle, disheveled and unsettled, through the halls of a narrative made of ghosts and Bordeaux. I hear the clink and jingle of Oriana emptying the dishwasher. I don't give this meaning. It doesn't need meaning. It's the meaning of itself.

Do you ever feel green with virtue? New to it, supple with it, sliding around in it? I generally stride toward it, assuming all and assuming nothing. But prepared to do the best. To think it through. Look chaos in the eye and say: do your worst and I will spring back. Things have value. We should try hard to care for them. Like those orchids Oriana received when she retired. The assumption is usually that these orchids were not meant to last. They're like cut flowers, the fragrance and prettiness of a gesture, a warmth, when the durable is awkward or uncalled for.

There are values that tantalize with their fugitive intimations. The idea that something may be true while other things may be false is a slippery, misleading binary in which the truth lies hidden behind a mountain of words, many of them well-crafted but daunting to approach. You can't help but admire the attempts. The intellectual thrill of watching words hatch their meanings in front of you, on a page, in a book, with the door closed and the chores done.

10.22 p.m. I get up to satisfy a craving for yogurt and blueberries. Oriana is reading "The Generous Gambler" by Charles Baudelaire. We exchange thoughts on Baudelaire's early demise. He died of a massive stroke in August 1867. He was 46. He didn't die right away but lingered in semi-paralysis, barely able to speak, for two years in various "maisons du santé" in Brussels and Paris.

I spend hours reading Proust. The sentences are like Piranesi's labyrinths, complicated stairways and arches and vaults and hanging pendulums, though not always. Sometimes they have the flow of music and are like those compositions by Chopin that create a pattern that is seeking resolution, and right when we you think it's coming, it doesn't come, it piles on more and more anticipation until, at last, it resolves in a thunderous waterfall of notes.

Reading complicated writers is like fly-casting. If you get a bite and miss, simply continue the drift and try again. Words as fish sip hatching flies off the surface of the water. Who's doing the hatching and who's doing the flying? The answer is hidden underground and is about to emerge and say something stupid. So, really, there is no answer, there's just these ties in the closet, and Marcel Proust. If I could live my life backwards, I'd begin right here. I'd start by attending more parties. Then go home and open a good book and think about all the things I might've done had I not already done them and found them a bit wanting, because other choices were involved, and there's only one easy solution, and it's a mirage at the end of the highway.

9.00 a.m., a bright sunny morning. I'm sitting in the car waiting for Oriana. We have to take our Subaru in for a check-up at the dealership. They need to take a look at the transmission, too. We're getting a big clunk from the transmission when I accelerate.

I like sitting in cars with the engine off. It's very still, and I get a secure feeling being enveloped in all that metal and glass. I see threads of gossamer shine out when the sunlight hits it, languorous and adrift. Oriana arrives and I start the car and off we go, clunk, clunk. I feel like something amiss in the drive-train. We wonder if we'll make it there. It's about a 10-mile drive. I go really slow and the problem disappears after a few miles. Something of a relief. We enter the dealership office and stand at the counter while a nice middle-aged woman itemizes what will be done during the servicing of our car and what it will cost, which is hefty. We sign a few forms and the woman strongly suggests that we also get the timing belt checked. Neither of us know what a timing belt is, but it sounds important. Also quite pricey. A bad timing belt can lead to big problems. Subaru engines are interference engines, which means that if the timing belt breaks, the valves and pistons may collide. Ouch. That sounds terrible. Our mileage is embarrassingly low – 28,000 miles or so – because we only run errands around the city. But the procedure is recommended, according to age as well as mileage. Life is expensive in the 21st century. No wonder we don't see artists in the city any more. I glance aside at the wall. There's a photograph of dogs sitting in a row on a canoe in a small lake, with a caption below that says "where no cat fears to go." I'm not sure what that means. That dogs are more intrepid than cats? I wonder how the photographer managed to get those dogs to sit there uniformly in a row like that. Or how the dogs managed to get the canoe that far out in the lake. "We all wonder the same thing," the woman behind the counter says. "We all think it's been photoshopped."

Hard to say what's real anymore.

We're given a loaner car with a computer screen functioning as a rearview mirror. I find it distracting, too much like looking at a TV. I prefer the mirror.

We stop for breakfast at an IHOP. Oriana gets waffles. She says they're the best she's had in a while. I get the works, sausage links, bacon, hash browns, eggs, and pancakes. I'm in breakfast heaven.

Oriana tells me about a guy who got sick of getting ripped off by mechanics and so learned mechanics on his own and became a mechanic. I often wish I'd become a mechanic. I like machinery. It's fascinating, how one part affects another part and everything works in unison. Just like language. A poem is a small (or large) machine made of words. Said Williams.

And what of time?

Time is synchronous and bald and everywhere at once. That's why the hands of the clock go in circles. You come back to where you started, amazed at the cherubs buttered with light.

And what of writing? What of the machinery of meaning-making? Or the oft derided Derridean machinery of linguistic autonomy, like those Tesla cars with Autopilot features. Language as a grammatological vehicle that functions best on those non-linear highways to the cities of *différance*, with all their diversions and thrills and deferrals of meaning.

You'd think, wouldn't you, that writing had a sacred origin, like ice age art? But it didn't. Its origin is a bit lackluster. It began with the Sumerians, whose cuneiforms were dedicated to accounting, not literature. Literature came later, after all the grains were stored, the bread baked, the people fed, the fields properly irrigated, and everything organized and accounted for. Then it was time to descend into the chambers of the imagination and visit the dead. Mystical pursuits are generally shelved until bodily needs have been met. The universe percolates somewhat slowly through the filtering structures of the brain. It's difficult attending to business when the mind is so dilated it takes a full half hour to button a shirt or do the dishes or oil a catcher's mitt.

There will be licorice and root beer in our conversation from now on, and together we will thread the air with melons and rattlesnakes. I'm going to offer you an invitation to stick around and wait for something to happen. That's largely what writing is about: waiting for something to happen. And if nothing happens, if the air surrounds you with a mocking stillness, you must learn to make things happen. Shock the air with a mad proposition. Hammer nails into your breath.

I grew up in an era of great musical discoveries and have been spoiled ever since. I expect the world to be beautiful, seductive, crazy and wild, decorated head to toe in jewelry and tattoos, humming a Rolling Stones song, and resonant with tambourines and jasmine. The bus is the best place to be when you discover that everything you've been taught is wrong. Late at night when there are a lot of empty seats is best. But when your stop comes up, try to get your change in the box without spilling it everywhere. Here I am on the verge of another faux pas. I've committed so many by now it has become characteristic of my general gait. I'm not a man, I'm a book. If you keep everyone agog and scratching their heads they won't be as apt to notice you just farted.

At some point in life you realize you took a wrong turn somewhere and now you're on the wrong road and so utterly lost you can't even remember your original destination. All I know is that when I pick up a hammer, I like to convince it that I know what I'm doing and pound the nearest nail into a chunk of wood with passion and deliberation, purpose writ large in my furrowed brow, my eyes full of Italy and volcanos and Anita Ekberg. Life is all habit and event with luscious moments of glorious fun. The heart is a thick chamber of blood. It's a powerful organ and should be treated with respect. Therefore, I have built for you a bamboo motorcycle, using only a hammer, a bag of almonds, a giant emotion, and a few well-chosen words, mainly the ones that fall out of my head, come tumbling out of my mouth, and hit the air like pistons driving the cost of ownership up and the euphoria of owning nothing as prodigal as ingots of sunlight.

I can think of nothing sadder than someone trying to speak to the dead. I get it, though: the dead know everything. Everything worth knowing. How does one ascribe value to a thing, a phenomenon, an event? What is the price of Being? Last night I saw capitalism die in a brothel. The play was *Pericles*, by William Shakespeare, and the woman was the beautiful Marina, daughter to Pericles, kidnapped by pirates and sold into prostitution. Marina's eloquence, delivered in private to each unsuspecting customer, spoke to the good, the true, and the beautiful. And it changed men's hearts. They left the brothel without getting what they came there for, but renewed, transformed, converted to loving concern. It wasn't long before Marina was lectured by the infuriated madam as lacking in team spirit and failing to fulfill her mission as a sex worker. Prostitution may not be for everyone. You must ask yourself: what wisdom can I share? What comfort? The money will follow. Of course, if it doesn't, there's always Sparks, Nevada.

I've never had what you might call professional detachment. I get attached easily. I'm like human Velcro. What I love best is the grammar of getting up to open the windows. It moves me like the leaves in June, so green and translucent that they seem like certificates of rain, contagious with intellect, and dripping little dots in the mud. Have you ever tried digging in Nevada hardpan on a hot day? Don't. Avoid it. Yes, like the plague. Hard not to say it. It's everywhere. Pandemic comes from Greek pandemos and means pertaining to all people, public, common. Sartre, on the other hand, said, as I said earlier, Hell is other people. That's a different virus. That's the virus of misanthropy. A lot of people enjoyed the imposed solitude of the plague, then they got restless. I got restless. So restless I surrendered to my shadow. And look at me now, will you ... walking this thin red line between Heaven and Hell. It helps to be flexible. When things go wrong, wrong with you, it hurts me too. Think of neurons as the dendritic roots and branches of bald cypress in a Mississippi swamp, synapses flickering with phosphines, soft blue plumes of methane aglow in the shifting mist, and the whine of a slide guitar echoing through the night.

Words are pollen, the tongue a stamen. If I see a solitary nomad on the horizon, I will know that man is me and that I'm dreaming. It's all in the qualia, the integuments and syntax of a universal language broken into digestible fragments. My brain and infinity don't get along. I like declamations. Explosions. Tap-dancing and Fred Astaire. Infinity is quiet and cold. I prefer the warmth of adverbs, muddy utopias and nimble superfluities. A bit shameful, really. Language should be used for nobler pursuits, law and medicine, not emitting blobs of molten glass, a big shiny loop of it floating out into space and making a fiery peacock dance in the window, which is also glass, and is part of the overall equation, the buzz of the bee in everybody's bonnet. Just remember, letters are instruments, and the predicate here is a black inverted heart, crazed as the ship's carpenter knocking on the scorpion door of your desire. He wants to build you something. A slug with a sack of drums. The incense of absence. The black of lack. The blue of you. And the taste of gone.

We all want a story. I know I want a story. But how do you make a story out of a single moment of perception? In each distillation of time there's a narrative persuasive as the music of two voices, a man and woman, combined in sound, emotions intertwined in sound, braided, kneaded, palpable as a wrist, that bone there, the ulna, right next to the palm, lush mound of muscle and skin. The story there is digital, in the literal sense of digits, from Latin *digitus*, finger, toe, spill of wine running down a bare arm. This is the legerdemain of digression. I'm not an undertaker, no. But what I'm undertaking is to be understood as an undulation. The story is in the ripples, the waves, the reeds, an infant in a basket. Women washing clothes in the Nile. It gets going after that. Exile and whirlwinds of fire. The sea dividing in twain. An oceanographer would call that an anomaly, a departure from average conditions, a wind setdown. Such occurrences have been observed in Lake Erie, also in the Nile delta in the year 1882, thus obfuscating the power of metaphor, deflating biblical cosmology with a surge of rationality, and dividing the empire of the imagination from the empire of the empirical, giving the lie to a predictable and mechanistic universe – Blake's Newton crouched, calibrating the strict limits of the real with a compass.

June 30th, 2022. The first night of what was to be the Eurockéennes Festival in Belfort, a city of some 46,443 souls in northeastern France, between Lyon and Strasbourg, got canceled by a freak storm, quite violent, that injured seven people and sent gusts of water shooting onto the stage like something out of *King Lear*. The madness of the weather: puffed cheeks of an angry God. Organizers, disorganized, tried closing the tarpaulins, but they flapped like the wicked wings of the air dragons, the roar of disruption. This is our world now. It's a time of madness and magic, a throwback to the dark ages when superstition reigned supreme and alchemists bubbled metals into gold in cold granite basements of grimoire and grim reckoning. And then they became poets and tried blazing the world down, which threatened no one. When people are stressed with the extortionate abuses of healthcare or rampant inflation or the threat of nuclear war, the poets are ignored while the evangelists fill stadiums and beleaguered politicians fill the streets with militarized police. And who wants to dally among unavailing lines of poetry when they're standing in incessant lines to fill out interminable forms for unemployment claims?

Oriana and I live in a region of gloom: the Pacific Northwest. A place of moss and spruce and cedar, mushrooms, fungus, and big slimy slugs. Sunny days are an exception. Most are overcast. Our small, one-bedroom apartment – which is semi-underground – is a cave. Oriana has been seeking an LED grow lamp for her orchid. The light in our apartment is so dim that the light meter app on her phone barely registered 500 lumens. Easier to grow stalactites here. I'm often tempted to paint horses and bison on our walls.

Oriana's employers also gave her a pair of plane tickets to the destination of our choice, $600 in gift cards, and four nights in a Marriott hotel. We exchange ideas on where to go. We decide Hawaii would be a nice interlude during the winter. We both have a craving to see the universe. We haven't seen a night sky full of stars since a trip we took to Long Beach, Washington, in 1999. There are lots of places in Hawaii unpolluted by urban light and good for stargazing. Also: warmth. Wouldn't it be great to wallow in warmth for four days solid?

Anywhere else? I ask her. Hawaii might be pricey. How about Deadwood, South Dakota?

I don't know, Oriana answers. I'll have to think about it. Anywhere warm would be great. The Caribbean, maybe. Martinique or Guadeloupe. I hear the food's great there. But the winter weather could be freaky. I worry about hurricanes, and getting home to our cat Molly. That said, I must say that sunlight and white sandy beaches sound fantastic. And clear blue water. You know, Oriana muses, they say a lot of people in the Pacific Northwest are gloomy because of the weather. I've got my own weather, I tell her. Partly sunny, with a slight chance for nihilism.

A computer once told me that I was shallow because I let the weather affect my moods. It was a friend's computer, so I didn't punch a hole through the screen.

According to French historian Alain Corbin, the history of sensitivity to the weather has become a major datum in the history of emotions. In the 18th century, notions of a meteorological consciousness emerged with force, the variations of the weather paralleling the vagaries of the self. The weather-sensitive person matches the state of her soul to the state of the sky. The moment she gets up, she checks whether it's raining, sunny or windy, and her day is conditioned by it. This inclination was born in England as early as the 17th century, with Robert Burton's book, *The Anatomy of Melancholy*: it shows that valetudinarians like to watch the weather.

At the time of the French Revolution, weather-sensitivity prompted some people to withdraw from the world. This would certainly apply to Oriana and me. We prefer our shared solitude to the hurly-burly of the social sphere in which mass shootings have become a daily reality (over 314 mass shootings so far in the U.S. in 2022) and people have become hypersensitive about everything from gender distinctions to the giddy excitement of provoking Russia or China into a nuclear war. If someone expresses concerns about a nuclear holocaust and the urgent need for diplomacy, they're likely to get called a Putin Puppet or a right-wing white supremacist. A city councilman in Oregon who was a little anxious for a meeting to begin was accused of being a white supremacist since urgency is a sign of white supremacy. No one need remind me that eight months after Louis the 16th was executed, Robespierre declared that "terror would be the order of the day," and in the ensuing months, during which France was ruled by a group of men called the Committee of Public Safety, 17,000 people were executed and another 10,000 died in prison.

Joseph Joubert, friend of Chateaubriand and Diderot's secretary, considered that our life, like that of clouds, is woven wind, implying a fabric of cosmic textures much larger and interrelated than the one circumscribed by skin, and sought refuge in nature to assuage the engulfing perturbations of the French revolution with the kind of enlarged perspective mountains and rivers can inspire. The romantics, too, found inner sustenance and inspiration in nature. Rousseau used the term "barometer of the soul." A barometer balances the weight of the atmosphere against the weight of a column of mercury. You can do the same thing in writing, where the atmosphere of the mind weighs itself against the mercurial vagaries of words.

You can take an emotion and mix it with some music and it will expand into vistas of unfettered feeling, the life of heart and soul. Music is a magnificent sublimating force. Music slips out the back door of semantic chicanery and exalts the spirit beyond the tether of all that is stale and static and acquiescent. Emotions grow large as experience itself. It's all joules and amperage. Immediate as rain. Hectic as starlings. Those kinds of emotion don't come cheap. They require a huge landscape, for starters, and mountains and buffalo, the kind of hardtack reality the tough old west brings to the faces of women while the men go around on horses shooting at things. Our local history will testify to this. It's all based on algorithms now, and low clouds and horsehair bows. The violins are for making wood sound sad, and that weird dark bottle someone put on a shelf way in the back, with all those boxes and sacks of dirt, was intended for something but no one remembers what. It gets like that a lot these days. Ideas come, ideas go. But the ones that stick are rushed to market before the next new thing gets here. And that's the trouble with things, right there. No one takes the time to package the inconceivable and send it to somebody, anybody, maybe in the text of an email, or stick it in a bottle and toss into the sea. Which is pretty much what writing amounts to these days, reveries sent adrift into oceans that would have made Ferdinand Saussure blush. Well, the whole thing was his idea to begin with. I just saw all these words lying around and kicked them into high gear, and a woman came along and did handsprings on them, and identified herself as a muse, and shook her hips and turned purplish red. Loose flesh about the lower jaw. A papier-mâché hat. Blue. Shooting sparks. Snapping a moral code with her teeth, she flew into the air and played a violin so beautifully it died.

I can't get the Tyrannosaurus Rex out of my head. It happened after I found out this giant animal had feathers. Trying to picture feathers on a Tyrannosaurus taxes the imagination a bit, I won't lie. And therein lies its charm. That way images have of getting into the head and squatting there until the imagination feeds it a nostrum of anything-goes, the go-to elixir for all things bizarre, yet real, as real as anything can be with acute vision, acute smell, and the ability to go long distances, thanks to the feathers, which help direct the wind over the body in a current that overall cools the animal down, all eight tons of it. It's always the things that have no existence that most capture my interest. Because all the fun is in giving them existence. Which is easy. And impossible. Impossibility is always easy. Possibilities are burdens. They need fulfillment. Impossibilities are pure energy. There's nothing to fulfill. No wheels to turn, no levers to pull, no tanks to fill, no pedals to pedal. Just an insanely verdant landscape to plant in your mind, a volcano in the background belching dark ugly smoke, and the smell of freshly eaten meat, and a soft warm breeze giving the magnolias sway.

I haven't said a thing about my chair. It's important. I sit on it for much of the day. For that reason, and many more, I had it reupholstered. The seat is covered with a fabric of olive green with golden arabesques. It's been a problem keeping our cat from scratching it. But apart from that, it's been a good chair all these years, structurally trustworthy and gracious. The arms are smooth, with a subtle curve. I remember the day we brought it to the upholsterer and we were all wearing masks and remembering to hike them up when they fell beneath our nose. Those masks could be pesky. But what a relief not to have to smile at everybody. It was as if my face were on vacation. I didn't have to bother with making expressions, I could just be myself. I wonder if a lot of people felt that way. It is nice to see smiles again. So maybe the effort was worth it and now that it's back it's got more energy because it took a nice two-year-long rest. I'm glad to be rid of the mask, but Oriana still wears one if she's indoors at some public venue like a grocery. Can't blame her. Two years of feeling threatened by something invisible is going to leave you with a funny feeling of uncertainty. Funny in the sense of odd. Peculiar. In all the millennia we homo sapiens have been cavorting about, it still feels unnatural to go about with masks. Masks are intrinsically theatrical, a covering expressing a distrust of the external world, a bit like the ones the doctors wore during the plague years in the 17th century in the shape of an oval with two open round holes for the eyes sealed by two pieces of glass and a powerful hooked nose resembling a long beak. They could also be considered talismanic, a summoning of spirits, the spirit of science, which is presumably rational. Or tries to be. The essence of science is the scientific method, which is what? Nobody really knows. Ideally, it's observation without presupposition. But good luck with that. The language, the instruments, the methods used all depend on clear presuppositions about how the world works. And there is much phenomena that cannot be observed at all. All one can do is try.

Nietzsche found the rule more interesting than the exception, at least he said he did, but maybe he changed his mind. I find exceptions far more interesting than rules. Or codes and conventions. Life is sweeter in the intervals, those places sandwiched between the general and the particular. Of particular concern are tomatoes. Oriana has been growing tomatoes. Shiny red spheres dangling like retinas from the skull of an earth god. How does one describe hunger? It feels like emptiness eating you alive, the merciless black in the eyes of a scavenger, flat empty plates of caked mud on a table. There have been omens, rumors of coming hunger. Oysters cooking in their shells off the coast of British Columbia during the heat dome of 2021, for example. Easy enough to feed the mind. One can imagine fillets of lingcod dipped in a light beer batter. The sizzle of a juicy burger. Blueberry pie under a mound of whipped cream. Mushrooms sizzling in butter. The mind is happy. But the stomach grinds away at its own membranous lining, cursing acid and fire.

I put two dowels in the grooves of our bedroom window so that they couldn't be opened all the way, even though they're at the bottom of a window well covered by a grill of black iron. The political climate is harsh. The country has become a penitentiary of militarized police and a skeleton dancing on the end of a rifle. Those of us who remain at the frontier of the inexpressible are sly and careful to not say too much. Anything overly abstract ticks like a metronome of impatience on the varnished shine of a grand piano. The subjective has become a swan in the ledger of the park department. An endangered species. Independent thought is demonized as self-indulgent. It's all about tribalism now. Hurling spears of insult on Twitter. Which, when the grid crumbles, will vanish like the sheen of spilled water on desert sand in Death Valley.

At night I remove my head and climb into dreams. Thinking keeps me awake, keeps me awake thinking, thinking about this, about that, how this and that are demonstrative pronouns which makes them eligible for rebellion, and this will make that look like a bicycle after we apply a little trigonometry to the situation. It's always a little amazing when you find a sound that matches your emotion, and this too is another indication that memories aren't dreams but have dreamlike qualities and should be taken into consideration next time you see a Zen monk fixated on a mobile phone at the airport. You never know when you're going to need a friend. There's a hummingbird and a song sparrow that've become friends in the park next door. The sparrow sings and the hummingbird hums and the music they make together contrasts sadly with the evident erosion of the world. I've discovered a new form of collapse porn: videos of Lake Mead and Lake Powell going dry. People walking around to look at the previous lake bottom and its many revelations, sunken boats and cement-filled barrels, stolen cars, lost cities, discarded firearms and human remains.

Let me ask you something: Do you feel that you're a different person now than you were some years ago? I know I am. I used to be wormwood and now I'm worthwhile. I used to be general and now I'm quite specific. I used to be predestined and now I'm indefinite. Change is extraordinary. You find, one day, you've become a guest in your own body. The mind changes so much faster than the past, the past can't keep up. Yet it's always weirdly there. No matter how much you change, the past keeps dragging behind, loaded to the gills with the lumber of rumination: remorse and guilt. You'd think they'd be pretty easy to jettison but they're not. They're like those Chinese finger traps that squeeze tighter the harder you pull to remove your finger. When someone tells me not to think of a banana, a banana pops into mind immediately. The harder I try not to think of something, the more I think about not thinking about it. A Möbius loop. They say meditation is good for that. I've tried it. They say if you meditate for a purpose, with the expectation of release from trouble or desire, you undo the meditation. One should meditate simply to meditate. Which takes me back to square one: a banana.

Intuition, I find, is generally pretty accurate, but it's hard to read your guts. Dreams are mildly entertaining, a little overly cryptic at times, but they're never too technical, and for that I thank them, and look to Jung for some answers. The color of an E-minor, he might say, is deep blue. If I embrace it, will it kiss me? It will kiss me with its octaves. Caress me with arpeggios. Destroy me with a cadenza. I believe anything can be brought to life on a sheet of paper – a monarchy, a boutique, a lyre.

Are you good at handling a crisis? I suck at it. Because we're having one. A crisis. Many of them. Crises. As in diaries. Places where things get written. Places where things get shouted. Shouted, then written. Written, then shouted. So that you can see the evolution, the rhythm and melody of things moving forward, moving sideways, but moving. Go. Find someone out walking and dance and hop around them and see how they react. Some will laugh. A few will join you. Others will look in horror and run away. And some will take a swing at you. Why do people fight? I've always been a little horrified at the prospect of punching someone. Not that I haven't been tempted from time to time. But it's not natural, not as spontaneous as falling in love with a humming-bird, or hanging garlands of indignation around the neck of a puppet. We all do odd things occasionally, sporadically, rain squids of ourselves on a stranger, eat raisins directly from the bag with a spoon, feel the massive weight of stone in Notre Dame de Paris as a testimony to the volume it contains, and the air, which is illumined by a thousand colors.

Neo-Expressionism in Cologne. Got to love it, right? I don't think so. I never did like it too much. Things change as one gets older. Which is good, very good. Nobody likes pasta night after night. Sometimes we want mashed potatoes. Pickles. I say flee the gallant cinnabar if it makes you zinc. The Hug King is molecular. Which means he can hug anything: the mirage at the end of the highway or the girl in the billboard drinking a Coke. Space. Time. The marmalade of quintessence or the space between life and death, which we call a highway. Nothing existed before the highway. The highway didn't exist before the highway. This is characteristic of all highways. They're doomed to get lost in the stars at night or lost in roadside bars during the day. There were a few things I noticed along the way. Important things. Things grow closer as they recede. And by the time they become so intimate it's all you can do to keep from collapsing to your knees and sobbing, and you realize the critical difference between a vine and a pan. The door is a species of architecture based on verdure. There's a thoughtful bear in the stern of a rowboat and the sun is sprinkling its diamonds on the lake. It's a good moment to remove your shirt. The nerves of the nipple are never dry but always inexhaustible. The land of ink is cradled in a lullaby of bedding. Feeling a beak establishes parables. And parables are palpable perpetuities of perspicacity. I was born the moment I heard "Like a Rolling Stone." How did it work out? A bit wonderful, a bit of loss and sadness, sometimes intolerable, often intolerable, but what the hell, there was a lot of paradise in between, when I could find it and hold it within for a while, so that I could feel it percolate, permeate my bones, and enter the blood and make me smile.

Oriana informs me that researchers have counted up to 100 million life forms in a cup of dirt. These range from microscopic bacteria (*Bacillus, Arthrobacter, Pseudomonas, Agrobacterium, Alcaligenes, Clostridium flavobacterium, Corynebacterium, Micrococcus, Xanthomonas, Mycobacterium* – they all sound like empires, don't they?) to fungi and pencil-dot-sized springtails and mites, to centipedes, slugs and earthworms that can reach several meters in length, moles, mice, rabbits in tunnels and dens. The fungi are really cool. They help trees communicate. A mycorrhizal network fungus connects trees through threads called mycelium. They also send nutrients and sugar from older, taller trees to saplings growing in shady areas where the sunlight is inadequate for survival. A study on Douglas fir trees at the University of Reading in England indicates that trees recognize the root tips of their relatives and favor them when sending carbon and nutrients through the fungal network.

Gardeners say that putting your hands in dirt has a calming effect. It grounds you. That's what the ground does best: it grounds you. Because the older you get the younger you get and the more you know the less you know and it's paradoxes like these that keep things from getting authoritarian and tight. I'd rather have chaos than a rigid order that causes people to flip out when you ignore its dictates and get a little reckless with your social obligations. People are nuts right now. Tempers flare. Everyone is at flashpoint. Hypersensitive. Thin-skinned. Entertaining all kinds of beliefs and superstitions. Observing completely irrational rituals. Wearing pandemic masks while driving a car with no one else in it. Wishing death and imprisonment on the unvaccinated. Some people cannot be vaccinated without incurring serious health problems. Doesn't matter, they should be barred from society. Because if you don't get vaccinated, you must've voted for Trump. And even if you did get vaccinated and had an adverse reaction, this is a clear sign that you're right wing, a white supremacist asshole.

One turns to writing novels when the world turns incomprehensible. You can plot a course that leads to a resolution, or an impasse, or Emersonian over-soul, or set things adrift à la Rimbaud in his drunken boat. The world doesn't need a diagnosis, it needs a boat – a big one, an ark, filled with books, baptisms, ballerinas and iced raisin cookies. Everyone is touched by tragedy sooner or later, except maybe the ones who fuss over moles in the yard and cracks in the driveway. That's a different, quieter tragedy, like the succession of kings in a tentacle of theocratic nails. The world abounds in assholes. Living artfully means finding strategies to outwit them. And this is what drives the novel to go underground and find a life among mites and centipedes, epiphanies in jars and planets in your soup. Heaven in a wild flower. Infinity in the palm of your hand. Hold it carefully: infinity is delicate. If it hits the floor and shatters we'll never find all the pieces. It would take forever to glue it back together.

I find bits of infinity in the oddest places. Tonight I saw a piece of it in our bedroom window, that weed that keeps coming back, and the way it glows when the sunlight touches its leaves: green opalescence against the shark blue background of the window well.

Determined not to lose myself in troubling ruminations, I focus on my breathing and let myself be lulled by Rosie Hamlin's angelic voice, which now spreads throughout my chest. "It's just like heaven, being here with you, you're like an angel, too good to be true." She died in her sleep of undisclosed causes in Belen, New Mexico, March 30th, 2017. I imagine a host of angels lifting her heavenward. Corny image, very Hollywood, but I decide to stick with it. I let it take form. I let it float to the top of my skull where it hits a stalactite and pops. Angels come raining down.

Plotinus said the body is inside the soul. Curious, that. It sounds ass-backwards. I've always thought of the soul inside the body. If you put the soul outside the body it becomes something much larger, atmospheric, like air and lightning, wind animating the trees and making them speak like a dummy on the lap of a ventriloquist. Some drugs will make this apparent. One must choose carefully. Avoid the grid. Avoid knives and rope, rockets and guns. Be intuitive. The energy holding the universe together may not be holding the universe together. It may be what makes things fly. Expand outward. Expand inward. Spend time in delicious idleness in a Lisbon bistro. What holds the university together is mystery. Dark matter. Dark energy. Cappuccino and grout.

"As with events, so is it with thoughts," Emerson observed. "When I watch that flowing river, which, out of regions I see not, pours for a season its streams into me, I see that I am a pensioner; not a cause, but a surprised spectator of this ethereal water; that I desire and look up, and put myself in the attitude of reception, but from some alien energy the visions come."

Everything I write is lousy with reverie. My elbows on the table, head resting in my hands. I feel punctual. But punctual for what? Oblivion? I'm an old man. But I don't go fishing for sharks. Dawn has other meanings for me than muscle and teeth. I feel like a guest in an aging body. The host is invisible, like an Airbnb owner. The energy, life force, whatever you want to call it, comes from elsewhere, because it feels that way, as if the wavelengths of a ravishing and animating divertimento traveling through eons of space began to engorge and diffuse within me. Tiny rips in the black veil of my field of vision let in a warm light on the other side. A crescendo brings with it a rapport with an oceanic consciousness. I become aware of the air filling my being, the slow sure rhythm of inhalation followed by exhalation, the systole and diastole of a universal heartbeat. I cling to this music as the walls of my consciousness begin to disintegrate and the black waters of the universe rush in, surprisingly warm and amniotic, and release me from the preordained grammar of time and identity, of maps and astrolabes and barnacled hulls in the mercantile lanes of the sea, of plotting sheet and passage plan, and set me adrift in those spaces Rimbaud described "where, suddenly dyeing the bluenesses, deliriums and slow rhythms under the gleams of daylight, stronger than alcohol, vaster than music, ferment the bitter rednesses of love."

I wore my colonoscopy socks today. These are socks studded with little rubber arrows and dashes to keep you from sliding, especially after a colonoscopy, when you're still a little woozy from the propofol and fentanyl. I walk on a carpet, not a varnished wood floor, doesn't matter, I like them, can't say why, I just do.

I hear a hullabaloo of crows and go outside to see what's up. The crows had gathered around the transformer that blew with a loud pop earlier today, causing a power outage for about 24 houses in the immediate neighborhood that lasted a little over an hour, and were cawing loudly and with great urgency. This must've been both a funeral and teaching moment for them. A dead crow lay on the sidewalk, directly below the transformer. I wanted to cross the street and check it out, see if I could recognize her or him, there's always a crow waiting for us every afternoon to get a peanut, hope it wasn't him. Or her. I can't tell the sex of crows. It's frustrating trying to identify them. There must be a way to do that. We can recognize the voices of several of them. The fluffy round head of what I believe is a male, who threw a temper tantrum one winter day, squatted on the sidewalk right in front of me and flapped his wings and berated me because he didn't get a peanut.

I keep wondering what will happen when I die. Will I become another organism, and if this happens what will I remember of being this organism? The brilliance of hands, the genius of legs, the silliness of hair, the agility of fingers, the clever opposition of thumbs, the weirdness of genitalia, the complexity and fragility of knees, the vulnerability of skin which, rather than separate us from the world, connects us to the world. What is the soul without all this? What would it feel like to be just that, an amorphous energy, a nebulous ball of effulgent cognition?

I watch a scene from a movie called *Certified Copy* in which Juliette Binoche goes to the bathroom in a quaint Italian trattoria in a small yet hugely charming village in Tuscany, leaving her art historian and estranged husband of fifteen years to fume over the disappointing quality of his wine and the cursory attention of the waiter, and deftly inserts a pair of dangly earrings in her ears and smears some bright red lipstick on. She intends to entice her disaffected husband into enjoying, at least for the afternoon, a little romance, some much needed affection. The tension dissipates a little with the application of the lipstick. Perhaps it will lighten the mood. She walks back to the little table and – not remarking or possibly not even noticing the earrings and freshly applied lipstick – the husband, still simmering in indignation over the waiter's negligence – to which has been added the nastily fermented resentments common to marriages that have been sabotaged by jealousies or infidelities or the slow burn of wounding remarks – responds unkindly and an argument ensues. I feel embarrassed and uncomfortable as if I were sitting in the restaurant, wishing this couple would quiet down or leave. It's always deeply sad to see couples arguing in public. And sad that the lipstick failed to work its magic. Women take such a chance with makeup; it's not that different from clowns putting on makeup. They're willing to make clowns of themselves, all for the sake of love.

What do they put in lipstick? The searing, misleading blur of cause and effect. Scraps of sidewalk radar. The rhetoric of thread. Ocean swells and the plums of paradise. But mostly wax, oil, alcohol and pigment. The wax is generally some combination of beeswax, candelilla, or carnauba. Carnauba – known as the "Queen of Waxes" – is obtained by collecting and drying the leaves of the carnauba palm, grown in Brazil, and is usually available in the form of hard yellow-brown flakes. Complex organic compounds are added and experimented with to give the lipstick its special character. So it becomes like writing. Words and phrases added to the general mass to make the lips seem pliant as ribbon when the words start poking out.

The skin of the lips is stratified squamous epithelium. The frenulum labii inferioris is the frenulum of the lower lip. The frenulum labii superioris is the frenulum of the upper lip. What makes the skin special is its thinness and delicacy compared to the skin of the rest of the body. Human skin in general is pretty freaky. The evolution of nakedness and our ability to sweat are unique. Skin is our interface with the rest of the world. It supports diverse and complex functions from protection to vitamin photosynthesis, thermoregulation, and communication. Every square inch of skin contains 20 feet of blood vessels, 100 oil glands and 650 sweat glands. It also contains more than 1,000 nerve endings that sense touch, pain, temperature and pressure. What I love about skin is the feel of warm, freshly washed sheets. The skin of Oriana, which is shockingly smooth. Cat fur. Sanded wood. The hilts of swords. The heft of a hardbound book and the solidity of its spine. The delicacy and flutter of pages in a book. The cold glisten of glass. A squeezed sponge. The mane of a horse. The brim of my hat. The prick of a needle. Bristles of a camelhair paintbrush. Buttons on a TV remote. Lichen. Balm. The vibrations of a massage gun.

A few nights ago I went to check on Molly, who was rattling the window blinds and hissing and racing back and forth on the sill in a state of extreme agitation. I suspect there was a coyote prowling around outside, and since the base of our front living room window is flush with the ground, it must seem to her as if the animal were right there in front of her. Our cat hates dogs. This was emphasized when we got her at the shelter eight years ago. I raised the blinds and tried peering outside and Molly – believing herself under attack - attacked my arm. She scratched it up a little, though she hit it so hard the bones in my wrist and fingers hurt. The following day, Oriana brought home some antibiotic spray from the grocery store but I didn't really need it, the wounds were healing nicely, and I'd poured hydrogen peroxide over it when the wounds were fresh. Not to worry. We should take it back. It's eight bucks. We stopped by after a run to return it. We had just gone for a run and I was dying of thirst. The day turned out much warmer than expected so I hadn't brought any water with me. We approached two women in conversation, a very young woman and an older woman who might've been her supervisor. The younger one led us to her check stand and began the process of taking back a returned item. She was a very pretty woman and strongly resembled Hope Sandoval, the lead singer of Mazzy Star, and seemed to be in a state of extreme depression. She did not say hello or attempt conversation at all. She worked silently. I felt like asking if she was ok. And she didn't quite know how to process a returned item. She asked for the older woman's help, who escorted us to another register. She seemed to be having trouble, too. She asked Oriana if she could highlight the item on the receipt. Oriana told her she didn't have any desk supplies with her. A security guard moved closer, probably because the till was open and full of money. Maybe he thought we were robbing the place. The item was processed and we were refunded our eight dollars. We went in search for water. We had some difficulty tracking it down. We found it in the wine and beer section. Outside, I unscrewed the cap and took a drink.

There's no comparable sensation to that of relieving an intense thirst. It hits you on a visceral level, Oriana and I agreed. That young woman at the register was gravely depressed. This isn't the first time. We're discovering disconsolate people at almost all the places we go now. They behave in the same downcast, listless manner as a population whose city has been taken over by a conquering army. They barely have the will to live. Meanwhile, the self-serve devices seem to be very popular. Most grocery stores only have one stand now. In France, they're called "Blah Blah" lanes, check stands for people who like to chat a little while their groceries are getting checked out.

Two years of social distancing will do this to people. Make them ill at ease around one another. The perception of other people as being potentially toxic cannot lead to good ends. It destabilizes society. It's not just a matter of germs. A difference in opinion can be as threatening as the virus itself. The hostility toward so-called "anti-vaxxers" was shockingly virulent. Even the eminently sober Noam Chomsky, a man well known and respected for his rationality, his razor-sharp analytical skills and strong adherence to the principles of social justice publicly stated that those who remain unvaccinated should be segregated, adding that obtaining food after they had "the decency to remove themselves from the community" was "their problem."

I think we, as a species, are lost. At what point in human development did it happen? This severance from nature, this deep sense of alienation, of feeling somehow superior to the other creatures around us. Was it this huge growth in consciousness that caused it? Was it a sense of estrangement that sent Ice Age artists down into the caves to perform their magic, hidden away from the world above and the herds of bison and mastodons, the horses with their sleek necks and gracile legs, and shaggy humongous bears ripping the bark from giant conifers in paleolithic forests, where the artists could experiment with this strange new power of representation in the secret chambers of a cave, in a sacred realm of fire and rock? And how did it become so perverted by industry and commerce? The planet is nearly uninhabitable at this point. The insect population has dangerously collapsed. If we lose the bees and other pollinators, we starve. Do we blame Descartes? Seventeenth-century western science? The people in our neighborhood have become so estranged from nature that the crows we feed freak them out. You can see the fear and animosity in their eyes. The idea of sentience in creatures they consider beneath our species angers and disturbs them. You can't exploit what you revere. The prostitutes and billboards on the heavily trafficked lanes of Aurora, a.k.a. Highway 99, testify to a lusty desecration. Our maladjustment to this planet is clearly a sign that the belief that we are – by special election – to fulfill a destiny of further propagation in the universe is utterly delusional, the vanity of a diseased intelligence. The fixation on a plan to multiply our species until the end of time borders on obscenity. The fact that we trashed this planet in the advancement of our technology is only further proof of our flawed intelligence and the great tragedy that entails. Those spaceships intended to carry us to other more habitable planets have not been built. They will never be built. The phallic behemoth Jeff Bezos built to ejaculate into space was done so at a cost of 5.5 billion dollars. 5.5 billion to float in space for four minutes. No wonder we're fucked.

It's true what they say about memory in old age: short term memory decays, long term memory grows in scope and lucidity. It seems compensatory. The world in which we find ourselves in our 70s and 80s is so extremely different from the one we inhabited in our 20s and 30s. Disorientation is symptomatic of a whole host of displacements, dislocations, discombobulations, and lost opportunities. An entire grave-yard of bad choices, misjudgments, indiscretions, and terrible decisions. Dead chimeras. Lapsed illusions. Perished hopes. The brain becomes a time machine. Think of a place and a time and voila! There it is, vivid as derricks on the Texas plains. That ugly sound of metal crunching metal endemic to car accidents. A bullet ricocheting off a rock on the North Dakota prairie where, at age 12, an uncle taught me how to shoot a rifle. Sitting at a small desk in the Hotel Arcata, 1968, reading William Blake.

I remember being 18 and new to California and growing my hair long and listening to *Rubber Soul* in candlelight and really loving that music and wondering why after all these years I hadn't learned to play a single musical instrument. Because I'd also discovered *Les Fleurs du Mal*. Different chords. Different frets. Different garden.

I asked a friend of 56 years if he had any regrets. He said no. I was stunned. How is that humanly possible? I could fill an Amazon fulfillment center with regrets. One of those regrets was not reporting back to a job in a Modesto cannery when I was 18. I went to San José to register for school and decided not to return. I'd spent a week crouched under a machine for peeling pears. My job was to hose the peelings that had fallen through a metal grate into a gutter that floated them outside the building somewhere. I could've called and let them know I wouldn't be returning. I don't know why I didn't take the trouble. I still wince when I think of it. My friend got me the job, and a place to stay. I still clearly remember standing in my girlfriend's garage listening to the Beatles' *Revolver*, which had just come out, the music of which seemed to give me a kind of permission to be giddily irresponsible, which in retrospect has wrongness written all over it. The Beatles worked hard. They met their commitments. They made sacrifices. Is old age a form of purgatory? Yes, quite obviously. Why else would I revisit those events with such punishing thoughts if I weren't trying to go back in time and redress all those errors. We're not the same people we were when we were young. You can edit writing, but you can't edit a life. And who, given such a power, wouldn't be spending all their time editing rather than living?

It took two failed marriages to get things worked out somewhat in that arena. No two marriages are alike. They have their own dynamic, their own particular synergy, and when they expire they exude a sweet poisonous odor, like oleander. The sex and intimacy that made cohabitation possible becomes poisonous. All chemicals have the potential to become poisonous. What makes them poisonous is the result of dosage. Marriage isn't a chemical. You don't see arsenic and grain alcohol getting married. Or do you? Music, wine and candlelight can bring about a chemical reaction akin to the volatility of nitroglycerin. There's a parallel. But it's ludicrous to reduce it to such. I know whiskey played a role. But I can't blame whiskey. I blame the wine.

The third marriage, my current marriage, is approaching its third decade, but still feels new. The more volatile agents were sublimated by an endothermic process of time, wisdom, and age. Endothermic means heat within. Enough energy to create covalent bonds, and find synthesis.

The marriage between language and truth is a very bad marriage. That one never works out. It's fraught with denial and recrimination. The marriage between language and reality is even weirder. That same discordancy between words and their referents, that same wonderful arbitrariness between language and the external world, applies to everything in the end.

What is the truest thing you can think of, the most stable, the most dependable, the most reassuring? Now imagine it gone. All at once. The rug pulled out from under your feet. That's what you call human relations. A betrayal. A look of absorption. A sudden unexpected comfort. A faith that things will turn out alright. Unsure footing. A mudflat. An estuary. Ask yourself: Who can I trust? If you say the Queen of England, you must be daft. If you say my lawyer, you are truly naïve. If you say my doctor, you are in for a big surprise. If you say my best friend, well, maybe. Friends have been known to be loyal and honest.

It's envy that makes things sticky. That's when the strangest resentments take root, conflicts impossible to resolve or put to rest. It's awful when wars between feelings use your viscera as a battleground. Even the brain backs off, it wants nothing to do with it. Meanwhile, the heart gets battered, punched silly into an enlightened calm. Bacardi rum. Comfortably numb.

Given the premise that all species, including humans, are here to reproduce and ensure the propagation of the species, I sometimes wonder why people are allowed to age beyond their ability to reproduce. I've heard of men well into their 80s getting women pregnant, but let's be honest, they're not going to be around long enough to convey wisdom to their progeny, show them how to build a radio or ride a bike or pass a football. But the thing of it is, they generally tend to be celebrities, rock stars, movie stars, industry moguls, and leave behind shit tons of money, which will certainly go a long way toward the education of their progeny. No, I think the reason we age so far beyond our reproductive years is the conveyance of wisdom to the society, which is why most leaders tend to have grey or white hair and turkey wattles under their chin. It is a treacherous world. If you want to learn how to be a gunslinger, find the oldest gunslinger you can find to teach you. This should be obvious. Staying alive takes prudence, stamina, and a really fast draw.

I put on my favorite pair of walking shoes and went to see the Fourth of July fireworks. Oriana and I walk up Bigelow, a residential street lined with chestnuts and cherry trees, to a vacant lot where a house was recently torn down, allowing a view of Lake Union below, where the barge for blasting fireworks at Seattle's perennial gloom has been set up. I'm wearing a cardigan over a shirt and T-shirt and I'm still cold. I regret not putting on a jacket. There are, as expected, groups of merrymakers going down the street to find a good place to view the fireworks. A few begin to stop at our spot. A large black SUV appears and begins moving toward us. This worries me a little. Does the driver see me? The driver is a woman, I'm guessing in her 40s, who sticks her head out the window and apologizes. She gets out and joins us while her two teenage boys get up on top of the SUV. We start a conversation. She recognizes us as the two people who go running every day and feed crows. She feeds crows too. I tell her we began running down on Westlake by the lake because the numbers of crows that follow us grew too large; this made some of the neighbors uncomfortable. Some of them complained about peanut shells in their rain gutter. She agrees that people can be a little irrational about crows. The fireworks begin but we can't see them. They're firing them off much farther to the north shore than we expected. We walk onto the lawn of someone's home, which makes me feel uncomfortable, although soon we're joined by many other people, which diffuses the transgression a little. We see a few crows fly overhead, panicked by the fireworks, and the woman tell us this makes her a little sad. I agree. I think fireworks are fundamentally stupid, but like a lot of other stupid stuff, there's something undeniably fun about them. I watch them explode into colossal balls of fiery color, like gunpowder chrysanthemums, and wonder if that's what the Big Bang looked like. I'm sure it didn't, but the imagery is cosmic. I wish I had stronger emotions about it. I used to find fireworks exhilarating. I've become jaded. A young Asian woman behind us shouts "Happy Birthday, America!" (she shouts it three times, hoping for a better reaction from the crowd, also because she's drunk), which, apart from its corniness, makes me realize how discordant the situation is: a country that is clearly failing, failing spectacularly to safeguard the lives of its citizens by using proxy wars to launder money, the entire government captured by a ruthlessly greedy corporate juggernaut intent on pillaging every square inch of exploitable soil and human labor, even to the extent of endangering the entire species and the destruction of a perfectly good planet, which makes the woman's celebratory ejaculations all the more ridiculous.

We both notice, on the walk back home, that the road looks different. This is due to the headlights of all the cars. The blacks and whites stand out more, said Oriana. It's granular, I remarked. The walk back home seemed somehow theatrical, like a scene in a movie. People in a celebratory mood, but since the festivities are over, and the next day is Tuesday, the mood is a trifle subdued.

It wasn't bad during the night. Nobody was setting off fireworks all night, as they usually do. I wake up the next morning feeling rested and relieved that the fourth is over and grab *The Wasteland* off the shelf. I often wonder why Eliot is so ignored by contemporary poets. There's his notorious antisemitism, but Pound was even worse. Why does Pound get a pass, but T.S. Eliot does not? I'm also aware that a lot of creative people are assholes. I separate the personality from the work. You have to. Otherwise, I'd be reading very few people.

T.S. Eliot always looks so pained in the photographs taken of him. He looks hypnotized by the moving texture of things, caught up by the feeling of existing here and elsewhere simultaneously. "Out at sea the dawn wind / Wrinkles and slides. I am here / Or there, or elsewhere. In my beginning."

They say civilization is a heat engine. I believe it. But then, I'll believe just about anything these days, at least for a minute or two, the time it takes to weigh a belief and see if it's worth keeping.

There are deviations to help get you through the day. A full moon in the middle of a hot afternoon, a cold gray rock in a clear blue sky still as a gravestone in a nearby cemetery. Coo of a mourning dove. I like those nicely shaded spots with picnic tables by the side of the road. It could be there. That could be the place. The place of elsewhere. Which could be anywhere.

Sometimes it's rejuvenating to hop on a barge, à la Rimbaud, after the haulers have been hauled off by some intervening force and go all *gangasrotograti*. This is a word I found in Nietzsche's "The Free Spirit." The footnote reads: "*Gati* means gait; *srota*, the current of a river, and *ganga* is the river Ganges. So the word means: as the current of the Ganges moves."

This is why I write poetry: every word is an explosive device by virtue of its superfluity. It's not required. It doesn't need to be here, to exist at all. And that's what makes it dangerous. The perfect antidote to utilitarianism. And money: the central tenet on which our entire system stands.

The space that goes from here to there is a cinchona. We're in South America. We're here by virtue of the imagination, which is by far the easiest way to travel these days. The instant you begin thinking about space, space opens up and there you are, in space. Outer space. Inner space. They're one and the same. Between is only skin. And momentum. It's a good moment for momentum. Don't let inertia stand in the way. Old-timers will tell you the mine is full of placebo. It's true. We've been mining placebo for years. They say it cures anything. Provided you believe it has value, and you were told it was something else, Special K or psilocybin. The shadows on the wall are skeletal figures miming bits of philosophy. Bring a grimoire.

I'm a nostalgia junkie. Not a nostalgic junkie, that would be something quite different. No, I'm hooked on the past. Sometimes it's painful. There are memories that make me wince. But there are memories that are important for reasons I don't understand, they didn't appear to have that much significance at the time. They're odd, non-consequential, yet weirdly impactful moments. Listening to *Rubber Soul* in candlelight, age 18, shortly after discovering Baudelaire, and feeling the first surge of Aufklärung smack up against my bones and fill me with divine afflatus. It's always a great pleasure to discover music on YouTube, especially songs I'd long forgotten about, but really enjoyed at the time, like that Danny Kirwan number, "Woman of a Thousand Years," which has a powerful pre-Raphaelite vibe, dreamy, wistful, yearning. Heavy with saudade, as the Portuguese say. I've noticed an increased interest in jazz, too, for some reason. It started with Etta James, and then progressed to *Kind of Blue*, which pulls everybody in sooner or later.

Jazz is more deliberate than rock, more sure of itself, because it knows where it's going, but doesn't know how it's going to get there, every step is important, the notes are lingered over, stretched out of time. Rock is staccato.

Tough. Certain in the way of football coaches. Until it enters ambiguity. All music is drawn to ambiguity, even rock. The full foliation of it, vines of sound coming out of trumpets, ingots of gold pounded out of drums, diamonds in a coal mine splayed into fins, undulations, an ostrich running out of a pseudonym in Australia, where names get wacky and there's topaz in the voice. Etta James at Montreux, 1975, singing "I'd Rather Go Blind," looks as if she's in a trance, or unbelievably stoned, but has complete confidence in what she's singing, means every word, the emotion riding on her words is genuine, and the music is a shoulder to cry on, and every tone, every timbre, a negligee in the moonlight, a glass of Chablis in the hand, and the full spectrum of emotion right there, woven into the waves of her voice.

It happened in a bar called Nowhere. I met a man with an ultramarine personality who told me that all the phenomena of life are singing off-key. From outside could be heard the beep of a truck backing up, the howl of the usual machinery, leaf blowers and military helicopters. I noticed a Remington hung on a wall opposite the mirror of the bar depicting a frontiersman leaning forward on a black horse, the ground covered in snow, the horizon a vast, ineffable blur. If felt as if one's eyes were swimming in a graphic apologue, a narrative elixir emphasizing how ultimately lost we are, but how attentive to details, how tenacious and unwavering, despite the evident uncertainties surrounding the human condition. This is why hammers are so compelling, and the mouth is a hammer of words pounding syllables into a semantic glaze of amazing grace.

I know the secret life of stepladders, I told myself. This shows that I can rip my life into paragraphs if I so choose, and it's a good to have a talisman or two about one's person at all times. Glitter favors the dullness of the bathroom. It's no joke to mock oneself in a dingy mirror. Pessimism is often a pyrrhic victory. What, precisely, are the connotations of the word "true"? Maybe you've noticed that words never actually touch the world. They run parallel to it, but in a very oblique manner, like a boat's gunwales in relation to the waves. Abstraction chews the world into structural pinochle, a card game played at one's peril. I can already feel the dissolution coming on, the disintegration of previous assumptions, the erratic progress of a handkerchief getting blown across the road. The indefinable churn of feeling during a heated conversation. I like it much better than optimism. What has optimism done for you lately? The very idea of Charles Bukowski makes me happy. He made drunkenness and desolation look redeemable and weirdly appealing. If it weakens the confidence of the brain in its fundamental beliefs, I consider a beverage a great success. An organ can grow into a public address system if the right combination of factors can upset the fragile equilibrium of self-representation by revealing other aspects of ourselves that are normally filtered out. I will emit misty hotel breath reciting certain poems, for example, or cause an old fever to turn on and transform the dull silverware of time into an arena of hummingbirds and peacocks. The glass makes small percussive noises when I tap it with a spoon. A certain time or place can underlie a reflective and narrative identity, but if we examine it more closely, it curls into loops and causes time to go backwards, like eddies in a river. We need room for speculation, the incongruity of a cactus in a rainforest, or a waiter whose solicitations are actually sincere. What does "noetic" mean? It means the menu is only half of the problem. Psilocybin may inhibit the activity of the "default mode network," but the rest is up to you.

I don't know what life is about, never have, though the mystery of it deepens with age. I do know what Nietzsche said is true: without music, life would be a mistake. I've got to have it, which is why we've got all these CDs in our glove compartment. An electric guitar is a burning actuality in the back seat of a red Camaro, a color that clatters with clairvoyant sunfish. I remember a time when you could drink from a stream and not worry about toxins giving you cancer or kidney disease or neurological problems. Water is everything, it's the new gold. Handel's "Water Music" was a response to King George's request for a concert on the river Thames. Did you know Beethoven was five foot four? Chopin was five foot seven. His heart is kept in a glass jar encased in stone in Warsaw. Dennis Wilson of the Beach Boys was buried at sea. There's an odd affinity between music and water. John Cage's "Water Walk," for example, a complex array of sounds involving a grand piano, a bathtub, a rubber ducky, toy fish, pressure cooker, ice cubes, electric mixer, and five radios. It was performed live on *I've Got A Secret*, February 24th, 1960, two years after Bobby Darin's hit "Splish Splash" and 10 years before "Bridge Over Troubled Water."

If you don't like something, you should shoot lighting out of your mouth until it shrinks back in fear and trembling. This will allow some time to find your calmer, more mature self, if you have one available. If you don't, that's ok, life will lend you a personality, and you can make a Buddha out of it, or a horse. Up to you. Entirely. Some stores still have a little white lightning on the shelves, and grommets and snow globes. They're going fast. People are upset.

I'm the kind of guy that if I ever met John Wayne and we got into a tête-à-tête that veered from the shallow neutrality of small talk into saying real things, he'd light up with hostile force, slug me, and I'd go flying across the room. Our ideas about life are so different, so opposed, so weird to one another, he'd look disgusted then walk over to help me up so he could smack me again. But I'd have a pistol tucked behind, and that would be the sign that things are getting weird here, I'd better slow down and rethink the whole thing. I'm never going to meet John Wayne. I don't even know why it came up. I grew up with westerns so I've got reels of them flowing through my head. It's entertaining, yes, but nobody likes getting smacked about by John Wayne.

John Wayne was not a worrier. That was pretty much the whole point of John Wayne right there. All American men aspire to this condition. No matter how tough life gets, however painful, however intolerable, you take it. You don't complain. You don't worry either, you take swift action. That's not me, I'm a firm believer in the power of complaint. There's an art to complaining. It even branched off into a musical form called the blues. And I'm big on worry; it's what I do best. Or maybe I suck at it, I don't know. That's a worry I don't have to worry about.

I worry a lot about food. And climate change. And crop failure. And the zombie apocalypse. I get demoralized every time I pass someone out walking who is riveted to a mobile device and paying a minimal amount of attention to their surroundings. Every time I step outside I see collapse. Western civilization taking a nosedive. There's always one thought that clouds all my other thinking. And this one is inescapable. It's stuck to my brain like mildew.

I watch a YouTube video podcast by X. I admire X. He's a very articulate man with a PhD in pathology from Duke University. He speaks with stunning lucidity on subjects related to the coronavirus, but also on a number of subjects related to science in general, with a particular focus on the oil business. His views on the coronavirus and recommendations for its treatment go beyond the officially sanctioned views, for which his Wikipedia page was taken down. He believes that oil – a finite resource, as is everything on our planet – is revealing signs of scarcity and this will lead inevitably to the collapse of societies globally. He and his wife have been feeling a growing anxiety which was exacerbated by a recent tour of speaking engagements. They saw empty shelves and a decaying infrastructure wherever they went. Each one of their flights had been delayed or canceled. The signs were unavoidable: the ship has hit the iceberg and is going down. He is somewhat cheered by some acreage he and his wife just bought that has good fertile soil for growing crops, a source of water, including a small hydroelectric dam for producing his own electricity. While he and his wife conduct the podcast, many of the comments in the chat group scrolling down to the right of the screen ask what about us, we're old, we're on fixed incomes, what do we do? Not one of these comments is addressed during the program. I find this disturbing. I hope X has an arsenal of guns and some children of adult age who are competent at using firearms. If he and his family are the only ones in the region with food, he will need to defend it from the thousands of people suffering famine and willing to do anything to stave off the pangs of hunger.

This is why I'm often advised by well-meaning people to avoid the news. But it's non-realistic advice. You can't avoid the so-called news. Which, if you're referring to mainstream media, is 100% propaganda. Complete shit. The real news is in the air you breathe, the water you drink, the food you eat, the roads you drive on, the bridges you cross, the forests you visit (the ones that haven't burned down), the grocery stores where you shop for the week's supply of food, those products that go missing, one week it's toilet paper, the next week it's baby milk formula, the pattern is freakish, there is no pattern, there's just chaos, fluky disruptions in the supply chain, people who have given up and are living in tents or their parents' basement, tempers flaring on the highways, mass shootings every day, 314 mass shootings so far this year.

Here's how I cope: I spew words. Like a spider, I create a web. Webs. Putting anything into space, however futile and silken and ridiculous it may seem at the time, does something, even if it just vibrates, things inevitably get stuck in it, and your web is a success, it's getting attention, which will lead to other webs, and what is the good of all these webs, I don't know, I started the metaphor but now it's here I don't know what to do with it except let it hang, hilariously ephemeral, as are all things in existence, an agreement noiseless as a library card. Next time a metaphor comes along I'm just going to let it sit there and wait to see what it does. Maybe it will become a great glowing sphere dripping with stars as it bangs its way around the large hadron collider in Geneva. Or a monstrosity of cadaverous reunion stumbling through a forest. Or the final stick of dynamite that will blow the tight grip of oligarchs to kingdom come. A cloud of words thundering with animus. A sanguine dish of worship. A Broadway show in bloom.

Paper legs traverse a field of lavender. I wear a shirt made of worldly nouns. My friendliness is round and my life is motley. I have a sense of belonging to a melody I haven't yet heard, but when I hear it I know that I'll belong to it, belong to the wistful drift of it, the perfect nonchalance of its resignation, its surrender to loss. It's a melody that comes from a distance, but a close one, a near distance, which is a true altitude, rhapsodic and glass, and full of Saturday, which kindles a craze for moiré, almonds in a kitchen drawer, and a sidewalk with a splendidly cracked narrative. I see a cat in the cabbage and a ticket to an Eagles concert discovered stuck behind the mirror. Clearly, the world is a weave of serendipitous frequencies, vibrations that swarm the head, all of them soaked in subjectivity, in furious musk, and hung out to dry.

And where do we go from here? Should I follow my gut?

What does my gut say? We're not talking to one another these days. We had an argument over some food and the subsequent indigestion did little to indulge my enjoyment of chili dogs. I believe in following one's intuition, but intuition can be hard to decipher as it speaks in the abstruse language of the cave, in which the light is dim, and the figures shadowed on the wall are pointing to their stomachs with a pained expression. Is that intuition? That isn't intuition. I don't know what it is. Something my duodenum dreamed up. They say our gut is a second nervous system. I'm not sure what to make of that. I'm sure my gut will think of something. People talk of theaters of war. Gastritis is a theater of bile and inflammation. And we know what comes of that. Those butterflies in the stomach before we go on stage or knock on the door of our first date is the small intestine sending us signals of new terrain, new feelings to digest. Synaptic chatter between the central and enteric nervous system links emotional and cognitive centers with peripheral intestinal functions, creating heartburn and war and mad old kings shaking with thunder.

Human desire has to be the most irrational thing in the world. When was the last time something I desired made sense? I don't want to gain weight, but this morning I had waffles for breakfast, smothered in butter and drenched in syrup, and found it satisfying. And I will probably gain two or three pounds. I'll try running it off later today, but for the sake of argument, let's assume logic prevails. What would that feel like on a day-to-day basis? Everything said and done as rational as a reflex, or a crater. Cause and effect. Life would lose its flavor. Therefore, we need trinkets, pastries, and inconsistency. Consistency is fine. For a while. And then it gets dark outside.

Desire is sweet when we meet what we want and what we want is available – oh, happy word! – and as eager and as

spontaneous in its gratification. Desire fuels our fulgura-
tion, the engine at our stern pushing us forward to new
shores, new experiences, new metals and metaphors, helio-
trope in a ceramic pot, citadels in the sand, our shirts
unbuttoned by the crackle of a fire.

It begins with a smile. A pensive look. A careless glance. An
usherette with a flashlight in the theatre of the heart.

Expression always leads to tears. Mine or yours, makes no
difference. The entire situation is monstrous, what can we
do? Someone is going to be elated, someone else disappoin-
ted. If there is ever an equivalency of feeling between two
people, the occasion grows merry, and there's an undercurrent of nervous distraction, because anything this harmoni-
ous must be unnatural, it doesn't conform to the symmetries of stability and order, everything in nature is catawam-
pus – if you don't believe me, take up wabi-sabi. This is harmony in chaos. The tandem of the random. Bare branches,
brittle seedpods, an old broken-down chair. Don't carry the
world on your shoulder. Put it in a wheelbarrow with a
crooked wheel, and a sack of rice.

Oriana and I talked about phantom limbs on our walk
today, the sensations that continue after the loss of an arm
or a leg. There's also the loss of people. This grows in frequency with time. You begin losing people in your late 50s,
early 60s, but when you enter your 70s most everyone you
knew is gone. And when I say gone, I mean gone. Gone
doesn't get any more gone. It often flashes into my head that
I want to tell my brother something, or wonder what my
dad thinks, or an old friend or professional acquaintance,
and realize they're dead. They're gone. Irretrievably gone.
And that's when you get a taste of the void. It's a real thing,
a real phenomenon. The abyss is real. There comes a time
when everything becomes tentative, a brown helicopter car-

rying beehives to another destination, developments displacing quiet meadows, ancient sequoias lost to fire, mountain villages washed away by avalanche, the glaciers melting with disturbing rapidity.

You learn to adapt. You read the Upanishads. The Bhagavat Gita. The Quran. The Agamas. The Old Testament. The New Testament. The Tanakh. The Talmud. The Dao De Jing. The Seven Valleys and The Four Valleys. Kojiki. The Egyptian Book of The Dead. Gilgamesh. Proust. Kerouac. Woolf. They will tell you what you need to know. How suffering fuels the spirit. Sorrow is the ultimate diesel, the most potent gasoline. Avgas. Ayahuasca. White lightning. A room with a view.

Confused? I'm always confused. I know confusion. It's a town, and I'm the mayor. Confusion is the medium in which I've learned to adapt using various strategies. Keeping your head low works. Hide under the bed if you need to. Works for the cat. Works for me. It'll work for you. Carry a compass. I wore a compass in Chicago and didn't get lost once. I just ended up in Toledo, Ohio. As long as you've got the right direction, you can't get lost. That kind of confusion is distilled into a single needle, and the chaos and jumble of life is sorted out by direction. Decisions are the hardest. It's always a pro and con game. If I do this, that happens, and if that happens, it won't be good, whereas if I do that, then this happens, and that would be problematical. This is what I mean by confusion, fusion is the con and the con is a fusion, don't make me shout, I'll say it one last time: I'm the mayor of confusion. I don't get paid. I've opened a million bridges and kissed a million babies. And I don't get paid. And this confuses me.

Bending has gotten a little rough lately. Don't like to do it. I'm not a river. I'm either horizontal or vertical. I prefer being horizontal until being horizontal gets wearisome. Then I bend. But only then: when bending matters. When bending has an impact. And if I'm vertical, I'm either out running, doing the dishes, feeding the cat, answering the telephone, or going to the door to get something I ordered online, which I do when I'm sitting, order stuff online, which is a form of bending. I like that form of bending, at least until my back hurts, and then I need to get fully vertical, become an Eiffel Tower of verticality. And one day I will be permanently horizontal. But if you listen close you can hear the word "horizon" in "horizontal." I love horizons. I love the fact of their illusory promises. The diaphanous lights playing at their edges. The fact you can never get there, to it: the horizon. The horizon just means there's an edge emerging in the distance. But there is no edge. There is no there there, Stein said. The horizon isn't even horizontal it's a wanton quantum.

I can't tell you where I'm going. But I can tell you what I'm packing: the roar of a lion, the heart of an ant, a hazy state of mind, a ping-pong paddle from the Mushroom King, a jar of equilibrium, an old wagon wheel, and the Gulf of Mexico. I'm bringing a sheaf of coconut paper, a fork of dark material, kneepads, elfin perplexities, a glass harmonica, a whisper of redemption, and a renegade glue. I'm folding a well of well-adjusted wet and including a fresh perspective and an inflatable debatable ornery cowboy hat with 200 brims and a bright outlook. I'm packing postcards, I'm packing it in, I'm packing a present tense and a mutating brick. I'm trying to get it all to fit. I have to use a crowbar. An elephant to sit on it. Click the latch, then I'm ready to go.

I've got these Bose wireless noise-canceling earphones. Being without that familiar wire is strange, as if my entire habituation had come undone and left me open to new misadventures. When things aren't there, where are they? I think they're in my head. The first time I discovered I could walk around with the earphones on and the music playing it was a tad disorienting. I felt like I was inhabiting two worlds at once. I can see how people get nauseous wearing virtual reality headsets. I can only handle one world at a time. Memory is a virtual reality and if I get too caught up in memory my mood goes for a ride in a merry-go-round of remorse. And what is it that makes any reality virtual? I've never met a virtual reality and I hope I never do. I like realities that are wild and implausible. The preposterous hoax that is the subjunctive mood will do nicely.

Life, said Emerson, is a journey, not a destination. If my brother could return from the dead, what could he tell me about his life? He built a house. He had a loving wife and son. He worked at Boeing as an illustrator, much like his dad. He wasn't a happy camper, I know that. He became glum in his later years. Much of that had to do with the failures of the culture in which he lived. Its stark superficialities. It's obsessions with wealth. Its need for dominance. Its terrible architecture. The cruelties it imposes on its citizens and the rest of the world, often accompanied by guns and bombs and extreme violence. I've heard it stated that had the country chosen the direction pointed out by its philosophers and writers, Emerson, Thoreau, Whitman, and Emma Goldman, it could've been a really great nation of compassion and wisdom, transcendent values that may have guided its industry and considerable resources toward a more elevated way of life. Didn't happen, obviously. When did it diverge? Before the Civil War? After the Civil War? And how is it that a country that can produce a lethal arsenal of nuclear weaponry can also be such fertile ground for poets like Allen Ginsberg and Diane Di Prima, Gertrude Stein and Muriel Rukeyser, Wanda Phipps, Marianne Moore, Gwendolyn Brooks, Gregory Corso, and Bob Dylan?

Franz Kafka loved to swim. Didn't know that. Just found out today. It makes sense. A man with an uncanny ability to embarrass logic with such eloquent intellect implies a visceral connection with a medium whose properties are as preposterous as water. Water is hypnotic. And perplexing. Water is the least logical of substances, yet also, in many ways, the most logical. You can see right through it. Yet it eludes easy definition. Who, for example, can define wetness? Or waves, which have the appearance of things, have a sense of thingness about them, and yet aren't things at all, they're energy, they're momentum. Technically, waves are deformations in any physical medium that propagate from particle to particle by creating local stresses that cause strain in neighboring particles. Which is precisely what writing is: deformations in the language that propagate from word to word by creating local stresses in the overall arrangement, or syntax. The result of which is the illusion of transparence by way of symbols, morphemes and signs, which are the product of brainwaves, and the slop of thought.

To relax the barriers on what is in your head might be induced by letting a hand relax the spirit of a tender curiosity on the convolutions of a vulva. Or the furious play of fingers in a Beethoven piano concerto. This is a nimbleness whose effervescence might otherwise be trapped in a fist. And this is precisely what the spirit of water releases when it pounds the rocks in a fury of foam.

Allow me to proffer something colloidal out of consideration for large molecules. Gels and emulsions, lotions and ruminations. The murder of mirth, which may be resurrected by touch, and encompassed by fat. Felt in the dark. Squeezed by a passion on the vinyl seat of a taxicab. The waddle of a goose on a dock on a lake. The sigh of exoneration. The music of conception. The insemination of language by steam and fortitude. Pounds of agreement pounded into a loving embrace. We will meet at the end, in a basket of song, with a collar stud and a flue.

Oriana likes going for walks in the morning. It's something she longed to do before she retired. The perfect time is between nine and ten. Most everyone has gone to work. The kids are in school. The streets are quiet. You can breathe. Linger. Relax. The birds are singing. This is when Louise, the crow with the bad leg, is most comfortable to come out and socialize and enjoy some peanuts. The streets in this neighborhood are fragrant. There's a lot of gardens in the vicinity. Goats beard, alpine strawberry, broadleaf lupine, camassia, blue columbine, Pacific bleeding heart.

How many songs can you think of with the word "street" in the title? Here's a few: "Dancing in the Street" by Martha and the Vandellas. "Baker Street" by Gerry Rafferty. "Where the Streets Have No Name" by U2. "Gibsom Street" by Laura Nyro. "Positively Fourth Street" by Bob Dylan. "Bleecker Street" by Simon and Garfunkel. "Street Fighting Man" by The Rolling Stones.

The streets and their cracks have so much to tell us. The movement of the earth. The castigating tread of tires. The beating of the rain. The silent scream of ice. The death blanket of snow. The searing tears of angels. The daily frenzies of commerce. The bombast of trucks. Bracelets of oil. Odysseys of traction. The mineral aggregates that create asphalt, that tear like the skin of dead theocracies, that forfeit that naturalness of dirt for the exertions of a forklift. A truck. An SUV. The gears of industry. The growl of appetite. The cracks are filled with tar, leaving squiggles in the asphalt. The squiggles are an alphabet, the runes of the road, cuneiforms of traffic.

We decide to go for a run along Westlake, where there's a sidewalk and a lot of little businesses and a few marinas on the western shore of Lake Union. The weather is nice, and upper Queen Anne is getting crowded. It's crowded down there too, but no crows to feed and no cars to negotiate. We stop at one of the viewpoints and watch a huge cargo plane fly overhead. It's the second day we've seen this plane. Boeing must be testing it or something. The plane is immense. The wings seem disproportionately small by comparison to the sheer hulk of the plane's body. It amazes both of us that a plane that big can stay aloft. That the same medium, air, that we breathe is the same medium holding that plane up. Not to mention the tanks and jeeps and troops that will be put aboard when it goes off on a mission. It will weigh somewhere in the neighborhood of 87 tons. 87 tons of material carried aloft by the same air I use to make words come out of my mouth. The same air that gives me life. The same air that feels so good breezing over my skin on a hot summer day.

There's also a yacht nearby, the Loony Loon, about 70 or 80 feet long, with three levels, sunbathing on the bridge deck and the stars and stripes at the stern. I imagine it's owned by a single person, which is strange to ponder when you consider the thousands of homeless living in tents here in the city. There's something profoundly fucked up with that.

Oriana informs me it was Nicky Hopkins who played on the Rolling Stone's songs "She's a Rainbow" and "Monkey Man" rather than Ian Stewart who played piano on most other Stones songs. Other pianists included Jack Nitzsche, Billy Preston and Ian McLagan. Stewart, who drove the Stones to their early gigs, also set up Charlie Watts' drums. "I never ever swore at him," Watts said.

I knew a drummer for a time in the sixties for a group called

Hypotenuse. The press said his drumming was a paean to pulse. He felt there was something imperative in the sticks, something urgent in the skin of the drums. There was a slightly off-kilter momentum to his beat, à la Charlie Watts of the Rolling Stones, which gave the rhythm a spicier flavor. He compared it to Legba, the Nigerian trickster god of language and destiny, who walked with a limp because he walked in two worlds at once. He said that it felt like something inhabited him, some spirit, and that drumming was an expression of that energy, a general all-round feeling of illegible energies trying to come out and show us how the world is truly made. After a diagnosis of arthritis he ceased pounding out rhythms on a drumskin and began dispersing his spirit-fueled odes in pixels.

Longing is a curious emotion. It's a form of desire, but a desire for something that cannot be consummated or realized. This makes it a very poetic desire. To know that one cannot have something, yet continue to desire it, gives it a certain appeal, a certain power. It's removed from the realm of the pragmatic and elevated to the realm of the imaginary. Things and sensations in the realm of the imaginary have all the allure and magnetism as the atmospheric play of light on a mountain slope or ancient city. Turner's paintings come to mind. This is where the intangible is given the tangible benefit of paint and the clarity of determination. The work of the will and skill of a painter to bring an essence into being, which is also that of the poet, whose words are removed from the mundane and muscled into paradise. But what is that paradise? It's the paradise of nothing. It's not even a place. It's an understanding, a reconciliation with the unobtainable, a futility resplendent with naked evasion. And so a mark, a notch, a symbol, a language substitutes for it and turns feverish and strange.

I've been all over the map in quest of *Sehnsucht*. The word emerged in some recent correspondence. I was told that the word means roughly the same as the Portuguese word "saudade," which refers to a feeling of longing, a nameless melancholy or nostalgia, but sweeter, way sweeter. This intrigued me.

I went looking for it in Rilke. I had a feeling I'd find it there. And so I did. *Du, unwiderruflich ausgesandt, gehe an die Grenzen deiner Sehnsucht.* "You, sent out beyond your recall, go to the limits of your longing." But I still don't know the full range of just how evocative that word might be, and I'm sure it's way more meaningful than longing, not that longing isn't meaningful but that meaningful comes in an array of flavors and colors.

"Angel Baby" by Rosie and the Originals comes to mind. I think it's that sort of feeling. Slow, enduring, fantastic and even a little fatalistic. There's a bittersweet undercurrent to the song, a feeling of death lurking around, a ghostly bearing laden with unappeasable hungers. You know that a sound such as this can't be played out on earth without repercussions, tragic consequences, splendor and haste. The emotion driving the song is so insanely wistful it's a little disturbing. Hearing it puts me in a garage watching two swaying teenagers enthralled by a nameless power. Its intensity is intoxicating. The kind that destroys worlds. And begins new ones.

And to think there was a time when music like that was an everyday occurrence on the Hit Parade!

Also out that month and year (December, 1960): "Are You Lonesome Tonight" (Elvis Presley), "North to Alaska" (Johnny Horton), "Exodus" (Ferrante and Teicher), "A Thousand Stars" (Kathy Young with the Innocents), "You're Sixteen" (Johnny Burnette), and "Poetry in Motion" (Johnny Tillotson).

So you see, I'm not nostalgic at all.

Music is a funny way to communicate. But is it any funnier than taking words out of their normal usage in conversation and making them pump semantic gas into the syntax of a Jaguar? And how is that different from music? With music, you fill stadiums, dinner theatres, high school gymnasiums, funky downtown bars, city center symphony buildings with chandeliers and champagne and oysters in the glittering, wonderful lobby. Without music you get weird looks, insults, accused of emotional terrorism: snob, elite, ivory tower butthole geek, all of which is true but veers wide of the mark, which is that music is a funny way to communicate, yes, but if you really want to communicate something, take off your language and put on some poetry.

No feeling is final – boy, that's for sure! I have feelings more than 60 years old. Some of my best vintage feelings come from the late '60s, early '70s. I pull those out when the current dystopia gets to me. People walking down the street, riveted to mobile phones. Tall glass and steel buildings where people with strange technocratic skills and searing analytical brains make large enough salaries to live in a podment. Scenes such as this make my feelings sour, and who wants that? I sure don't. You can give those feelings to the seagulls. Or pigeons. Or toss them in a dumpster. Or use them to clean the stove. The feelings I like to resurrect are those initially charged by oceanic vistas in exotic locations, the ones where the world appeared phantasmal for a few minutes and nobody talked about babies or football. Where nothing smelled of urine. Or laboratories. Or the scented oils of luxurious salons. It smelled like onions. And sounded like ducks. And felt like saltwater. And fire. Big roaring fires. And Joplin and rum.

There it is. It was there the whole time, I just didn't see it. I didn't smell it or hear it or taste it or touch it, but it was there. No, it wasn't parsley. Or a pentagon. Or a pentameter sonnet with rhyme and wallpaper. That wasn't it. This is it. It is what it is, as people like to say. Make of it what you will. It's yours now. All of it. The bits of it. The itch of it. The identikit in its itinerary of tin and potato skin. Its waterfalls and peccadillos. The Watteau of it. The platypus of it. The sheer balderdash of it. You can applaud it. You can encourage it. But until you find out what it is it won't go anywhere or do anything. You can think of it as wet. But if you want it as it truly is you must forget everything you've known about itemization and trust your instincts and put it here, pal. Lay it out where I can see it. The quiddity of it. The validity of it. The infinity of it.

Oriana returns from Costco with a bag of something called Orchid Media. I find this interesting. Do orchids have a panel of orchids commenting on all things relating to epiphytes? What's going on in epiphytic culture these days? The ingredients which compose the so-called "media" are medium fir bark, coarse perlite, charcoal, chunky peat or sphagnum moss. Tasty. If I were an orchid, I'd find that delicious.

Media is, of course, the plural of "medium," whose original meaning, in Latin, designated "the middle, midst, center or interval." Many of the secondary senses, which first emerged in the 1590s and have continued to evolve, refer variously to an intermediate agency, channel of communication, psychics, fortune-tellers, the stuff needed to create art (paint, clay, language, texture, drugs, drums, dreams, feelings, machines, expeditions), or the array of conditions informing any particular moment (rocket launch, poetry reading, funeral, wedding, road rage, swashbuckling, browsing used bookstores or designing aquariums). The word "media" probably arose from the term "mass-media," a technical term in advertising which popped up in 1923. The imagination is a medium of random encounters. Behavior is the medium by which expression finds its bellows and blooms. Expression is to behavior what animals are to the environment. Expression needs a medium in which to express itself in the same way birds need air to fly or fish need water to swim. Air creates birds. Water creates fish. Birds eat fish. Fish eat birds. Words create thought. Thought eats words. Words eat thought.

When we refer to mainstream media we mean an agency of propaganda that spews whatever narrative the governing powers feel should sway and motivate the public to conform to its liking. It works beautifully. Just look at those people at their big shiny desks with their confident poise and gleaming teeth and perfect diction. These are the bromeliads of the power structure.

Media expanded to imply environment. Wonderfully vague word, "environment": surroundings or condition in which living entities draw their sustenance and character. Environment shapes appetites and behavior. Conditions condition the volition of the zoning commission.

In other words, medium – or rather media – became the soft, loose, friable, moist, well-draining soils with a high limestone content and even percentages of sand, silt and clay in which we find the truffle. And in spiritualism, the medium becomes a human being with the ability to communicate with the dead. The environment of the dead is a mystery. Cemeteries are mediums of worm and granite and bone. Epitaphs and moss. But the realm of the dead is beyond the reach of human cognition. Nobody wants to go there, though we are told by those seemingly in the know that it's a paradise in which we are immersed in the endless oceanic love of a benign intelligence.

What do you like best, streets, boulevards, avenues or roads? I have a preference for roads. Roads are interesting. They tend to be gravelly and go places where there is ample solitude and adequate quiet to hear the music of birds, usually whippoorwills, sometimes magpies. Streets are stressful. Streets are busy. Streets are made of asphalt or macadam and often there are either too many signs, which is confusing, or not enough signs, which is also maddening. Streets require a lot of stopping and starting and people at the side panhandling and misanthropes shouting at demons and people vomiting and shitting and selling things. Boulevards are nice, usually treelined and curvy; there's a little more personality and a sense of ease, and museums, and stately mansions. Avenues are the same as streets but grander, wider, and lined with trees. Why do I bring this up? No reason. They're part of life, that's all. If you've got a place to go you'll want to use a road or a street or a boulevard or an avenue. I recommend walking, and taking an umbrella and a good map. I want to be of use, I want to bring some information into the highways and byways of life. We should talk about highways. Highways are better than freeways. Freeways are nightmares. Take a highway, preferably a main artery, a passage through time and space, a wormhole or interstate.

There are no streets or boulevards or freeways or interstates or roads for the human mind. If a mood ceases to vary, its duration ceases to flow. The mind isn't asphalt, it's water.

Two monks are arguing about a flag. One says, "The flag is moving." The other, "The wind is moving." A third walks by and says, "Not the wind, not the flag; the mind is moving."

How can anyone tell a story when things change so rapidly from second to second? The story barely gets started before things change, perspectives shift, new perspectives emerge, objects mutate, moods alter, expand, dilate, crystalize, melt. This is all the more so with the interior states, sensations, affections, desires, etc., which do not correspond, like a simple visual perception to an invariable external object. Or even a sequence of events, like my face looking back at me in the bathroom mirror, or a diamond ring stolen by a spider monkey. Yesterday, I saw someone's mind rolling down the street. It bumped up against a hemlock and wobbled a bit before coming to rest. I happened to run by the next day, took a look and noticed it was gone. Maybe I'll see a poster for a lost mind stapled to a telephone pole. Everyone is losing their mind these days. They thought censorship would help – it didn't. It made matters worse. Propriety collapsed. Oh well. Walking on water wasn't built in a day. Who said that? Kerouac? Yes, Kerouac. His response to some psilocybin, January 1961, at 170 East Second Street in the East Village, with Allen Ginsberg and Timothy Leary. It was muttered while looking out the window.

So there has to be some stability, yes? How otherwise would we avoid total chaos? Study the frets on a guitar neck: this is what keeps chaos at bay. The silences between the notes. The void behind the words. Each word refers to something not there, not here, and so the absence bleeds into the present bringing a stillness to the anguish pounding in the head. Form is emptiness. Emptiness is form. Empty mirror, unstained by thought. Frets are strips of metal, generally an alloy of nickel and brass. Vibrations between strings produce sounds that soothe the mind into welcome nullity.

Those moments when we allow ourselves to step outside of time are wonderful. Step outside our usual routine and do something that has no purpose other than personal enjoyment. Time persists, it's still there but it's forgotten, it's on a shelf in the refrigerator like a jar of pickles. We move to the interior of ourselves when the pressures are off and we don't have to compete for attention or perform a service and try to appear eager to do something for a boss or a supervisor. It's all an act. It's one of the first things you learn in life: how to disguise your true nature. Being artificial protects the content inside: the real stuff, the real treasure, the real you! Your reality. Let that out and things begin to rock. The boat wobbles. Things grow apprehensive, alert and unsure. You find yourself craving a life elsewhere. Even though elsewhere is always there. You just flip your schtick from disguise to speaking your mind.

The danger of artifice is losing sight of the artifice. When the artifice is so successful that it brings you rewards, it ceases being a tool and becomes a tumor. It eats you up. People worry about being negative. Negativity is hard to be around. But pretending to be all happy and smiley and shiny like some demented employee on a hot day at Disneyland is toxic. Let's get real.

For years, for decades, for my entire life, the future was a destination in time in which everything got better, devices made life more convenient, cars grew more luxurious, food became more abundant, there were fewer wars, less crime, more stable governments, etc. Of course, the opposite came about: as time passed more things got lost. There was less food, less potable water, less arable land, storms and floods became more frequent, more intense and disastrous, there were fewer products available, prices kept rising at a dizzying rate due to inflation, corruption in business and politics became the new norm, there were homeless encampments everywhere, censorship and the repression of dissent was aggressively maintained and expanded. When I talk of gone, a gone world, a gone humanity, a gone culture of creativity, a gone sense of security, a gone social environment, this is what I mean. What's gone is a memory of unsullied leisure, intervals of purposeless, unstructured time. A few of the younger set are smart enough to realize that something is missing, something nameless and noncommercial that made life more than tolerable, made it good. That sense of rightness that even animals have, the natural empathy that is a deep abiding feature of all living organisms, has been corrupted and distorted by competitive and opposing forces that lie deep within the collective unconscious – like something in the cellar of a derelict building, idle, forgotten, inert, a mound of forgotten midden under a dirty tarpaulin. But since it can't be killed, it remains a danger. Because once it awakens there will be hell to pay. And it will awaken, that's inevitable.

Why do these things bubble up? What is the point to them? How do they serve the unfolding of a new perspective? Am I looking for a renaissance? Hell yes, I'm looking for a renaissance. One is never too old for a renaissance. Magnificence, pathos, flaming pigments and madcap jesters juggling the skulls of tyrants.

Time progresses, things change, everything is in constant flux, but there is a core sense of being that glows from within like a sun, which is called the soul, and is a thing of great dexterity and art. Where there is a fluidity of fleeting shades which encroach on each other in human consciousness, the soul sees distinct and solid colors, strung together like the varied pearls of a necklace. The soul is then forced to imagine a thread, no less strong, that is capable of holding a set of beads together. That thread is a sentence. We thread pearls of sound together on a thread of syntax, dangle it in the air, and laugh that it has no reality.

Prose is three-dimensional: width, breadth, height. Poetry is four dimensional: tambourines, reindeer, underground comedy acts, and Hudson Valley applejack.

Our interactions with the world are reflected in our grammar.

I sip some coffee. The coffee is good, hot, dark and bitter. I hear a car. It roars by. The car is a mechanism for transporting one's body from point A to point B. Coffee is a mechanism for transporting the mind from dullness to stimulation. I hear Oriana cough in the bathroom. As I shift my body, the springs in the bed squeak. I don earphones and watch the news. Two bodies were picked up yesterday in downtown Seattle, victims, ostensibly, of a fentanyl overdose. The human condition is in crisis. Despair crawls into itself. You can mock the optimistic, but not the dead. The mockingbird is a plain-looking bird with thin legs and a slender body whose songs are often mimetic. Hence, the mockery of the mockingbird. Emulation or satire, the overall repertoire is enormous. Sharp rasps, scolds and trills. Charlie Chaplin spinning a cane.

According to the most widespread opinion, that is to say according to the implicit rules according to which we construct our sentences, the subject is the king of the action. It is what decides the action, carves the pumpkin, stirs the soup, fills the air with song and inflates it with meaning, shows us the money, fills us with joy or anguish, plays the violin, blows in the wind, builds pyramids, rotates blades, and pushes a large, heavy rock up a hill only to have it come tumbling back down.

The subject is exterior to the verb. It maintains a certain distance with it. It activates it from outside. It behaves like a stable entity and appears to have greater reality than that of the action, which could take place or not, and doesn't really have any substance or consistency of its own, given that it's only a pure movement, an outcome of what the subject is up to. But isn't this backwards? Wouldn't it be more illuminating, reflect our condition more accurately, to affirm that the human subject is never entirely sure of one's identity or intent and is inherently indecisive and fluctuating, a cloud of conflicting ions, and that it is action which congeals that mist into definition and form, Prometheus unbound, monarch of gods and demons and all spirits?

Scorn and despair: these are the burdens of my empire. Yet I endure. But who's the real protagonist here? It's not "I" it's "endure." Endurance is the buggy we need to get around the empire, subverting its murderous goals and whistling a merry tune.

By shaking up the grammar a bit, couldn't we give ourselves the possibility of loving life more? Rearrange our perceptions. Smear paint, rub the body with oil, I feel fine, I feel herds of words fill the skull with crying gulls, blooming onions, undulant crawl, paper spasms of hectic meringue.

Gertrude Stein does it best: successions of words are so agreeable. It is about this. Might which is folded. Disturb seemly. Anything that is why then may give them a share. Of feeling like it.

It is jouissance that allows me to say "I" in a particular way at a very precise point in space and time. Je est un autre. It took four words for Rimbaud to flip subjectivity into objectivity. I applaud his initiative but remain perplexed by his ensuing career choices. And silence.

This reversal of the logic of grammar also applies to sentences where the verb does not designate an action but has the status of a simple copula, as is the case for "being" in these formulas: "I am sad." "I am melancholic." "I'm opulent and hospitable." "I'm constantly inconstant." "I'm openly pyrotechnic and inclined toward strange deformations which help define the moment."

As long as the copula is considered as a simple glue, an adhesive force between two blocks – the self on one side, sadness or happiness on the other – it maintains an impassable gap between them, creating a partial collage. But reverse the field of forces and "I'm happy" or "I'm sad" no longer means I'm experiencing a mood, but that the mood is the force allowing me to taste this moment in space and time. It's the energy moving through me that brings me into existence.

Meaning: grammar is the hammer hanging from a worldly belt. Nuts, ovum, bags of plaster. Broken norms, bratty girls, flawed facts. Greek tragedies, indecipherable coefficients, old letters in perfumed boxes. Sonnets written with hornet ink. A lawn of powwow. A photogenic attic steeped in seismic glitter. A parcel of fire. Dinosaur tracks discovered in a dried-up riverbed. Sugar roaring at the polar crust of a windshield pedestrian. Go heal the air with your breath.

I like leaving the door half open at all times. I don't like a closed door. Unless the cat becomes a nuisance. These messengers of the unconscious crawl into the narrative to warn us of time.

One must be careful in discussing the past. It is fully manifested to us by its thrust, those memories that spring into being at odd moments, triggered by God knows what, a perfume, a cookie, the way the afternoon light brings out the textures on an old street, a mortuary passed on the way to Home Depot, or a mere tendency to drift backward, let yourself get whirled around in an eddy like a mezzo-soprano floating down a river in an inner tube, too drunk for opera, but sober enough to quote Nietzsche. Only a small part of it becomes representation. The rest are 45s in a jukebox in a Montana bar that get played once a month by the ghost of Richard Brautigan.

Every moment of perception is a creative act. And to this extent, we create ourselves. It's a never-ending project. And just as a painter's work is formed or deformed – modified, distorted, refashioned, reshaped – so each of our states is altered, bringing a new cast to our being, a fresh transmutation, a new metal forged in the heat of remorse or a glass engorged with the breath of a new understanding. It may not be anything big, nothing dramatic, but maybe something subtle, a new inflection, a new understanding of what it means to exist, and what the word "existence" itself entails. I say this while trying to work out my own struggle with the past, the way I behaved in the past, and how I wince to think of it. I wonder how many people doing time behind bars find means to change, so that the person being punished no longer exists. But does that release the person from the responsibility of the crime that put them behind bars? Am I fooling myself to think that a person can change so radically that they could emerge from a chrysalis with multicolored wings, their former existence as a worm completely forgotten? I often wonder – inspired by that scene in Star Trek Into Darkness where the elder Spock (Leonard Nimoy) meets his youthful self (Zachary Quinto) – what advice I'd give my younger self. Would I resent that older incarnation intruding on me? Probably. It would be like someone handing you a canvas on which a drawing or painting has already made some progress. What a drag.

This is the time of year when tiny mounds of fine sand begin to appear between the cracks in the sidewalk. This is the work of ants. Whole civilizations of them beneath the concrete. A world that is separate, yet critically involved, with ours. Their tunnels carry water, oxygen and nutrients to plant roots. And they help things decompose, which helps clean the environment.

That word again: environment. I've been hearing it a lot

these days. It's in trouble. Though actually we're the ones in trouble. We need everything the environment has to offer in order to stay alive: heliotropes, marshmallows, bedspreads, shillelaghs, wedding rehearsals and ants.

I love ants. I think they're great. What's not to like about a creature with two stomachs, spiracles for breathing, antennae for smelling, feeling, and touching what is ahead or behind them as they crawl, and to communicate with other ants. Ants have the largest brains of all insects. They have the ability to do complex navigation, domesticate aphids for farming, and lift 50 times their own body weight. The Asian weaver ant can lift 100 times its own mass. Ants' muscles have a greater cross-sectional area relative to their body size compared to other animals. So I admire them. When I see an ant carrying a crumb across the concrete with intent in its antennae and manifest destiny in its mandibles, it's like watching a brain surgeon concentrate on a neuron, or a welder shower sparks from the Eiffel Tower, or a photo of Samuel Beckett at his writing desk.

Whenever I see one, I see it's busy. Ants are constantly busy. They seem to have no capacity for idleness. This, I believe, is a serious character flaw. Idleness is essential to maintain the finer values a society can produce. "Produce" may be the wrong word. How do values come into this world? How are values lost? Values fade when the sensitivities of the citizens become blunted. Values emerge when the awareness of a society grows according to the voices and passions of a people newly awakened to the possibilities of life. Idleness being at the very top of the list. Idleness is a source of reverie. Reverie is a source of invention. Inventions lead to an enhanced way of life. Ergo, hurray for the idle for they maintain the organs of our dalliance and the glaze of our gaze.

Our cat is constantly trying to get me to meditate. She invites me into the room by the kitchen and sits. She doesn't want food or to play. She doesn't want her belly rubbed. She just wants to sit. And me to sit with her. And do nothing. Just sit. Sit and stare at the air. She really likes this. I've seen cats do it a lot. Just sit and stare at the air, like feline Zen monks. I really should've named our cat Zen, then I could say things like "I have to feed Zen" or "Zen bit my leg" or "Zen woke me up" or "Zen wants me to sit and stare at the air." And so I do. I comply. Cats love compliance. Especially when they sit and stare at the air. They like it when you join in. It adds something. Nothingness, I think. You can't have something without nothing and you can't have nothing without something. My cat said that. With her eyes. In total silence.

You hear a lot about the present lately. How being in the present prevents gloom and rumination. How being in the present keeps you from worrying about the future. How it slows time down, reduces stress, heightens awareness. It's hard to be in the present, fully there, fully immersed in the present. Like Gertrude Stein in *The Making of Americans*. Like a fire in the glow of a log. I find the present impossibly slippery. Changes occur in microseconds. And change is the antithesis of the present. Or maybe I'm misrepresenting the present. Maybe I don't understand the present. The present is present to me now. Now it isn't. It's gone, replaced by another present. This one. Which is now in the past. Or the future of this present. Which doesn't exist. So there. No reason to worry about the future. It's not here. It's not there. It's not present. And it's not what I expected. It didn't take long. I couldn't see it, then I did, and then it was gone.

And sometimes I can feel the machinery of language jingle and jangle as it attempts to lift something into the air. Something heavy. Something elusive. Something whose fugitive nature gives it the weight of air, which is heavy as the pigment it carries, the grotto it opens to a fracas of birds, the glitter it gives to the forecast of the harbor and the goats guzzling water and the pirates loading their ship. You can hear this in the greasy chains of ragtime and the glistening fruit in the jabber of women. The pharaoh of the pharmaceuticals and the shoulder blade lapping at the miscarriage of time. The convenience of gauze. The fire in the momentum of a horse. The smell of burlap in the smell of a piebald barn. Hips in a rhythm. Legs in the water. Hands on a table. Eyes hoisting a gymnasium of words to the brain. Succulent requisitions. Deliberate spurts of feeling on a violin. Reckless TV sitcoms. Spectacular polymers. Scalloped spuds. And birds in the rain.

Imagine a household of daughters anxious to go somewhere. Imagine there's no heaven. Imagine that John Lennon is entering the room in a black hat and a parakeet on his shoulder. Imagine the dead have risen from their graves and are dancing to ZZ Top on top of a big red truck. Imagine means to put an image in the mind. Form an image. Make an image. Here comes an image. Can you imagine this image? It's the image of an infringement in the sand. The infringement of the sea. Water rising in a sheet of foam. Millions of bubbles. Fireflies in a turbulent swirl around an old piano. Now imagine the secret in the back of your mind walking out of your mouth in a string of words and glowing like the heart of the universe powering a ghostfish in a grammar of undercurrents. Imagine all the daughters are gone. Imagine the shelves. Imagine the curtains. Imagine the quiet. Where have they gone? Whose daughters are these? They're here at the insistence of something. The clamor of these words. These crystals. These pistols. These curses.

Is it possible that something unnecessary is necessary

because it's unnecessary? Is sport necessarily unnecessary? Or unnecessarily necessary? Is art urgently unnecessary or blithely superfluous like names and birthdays? These and other questions invade the bric-a-brac of days.

Trying always to be rational is irrational. Ask a nomad. If a metallic shaking is lifted on the tongue, the sky will walk into a hornet and slip on a rug. This will result in a Texas of black angels. An undecided dragon hovers over Houston. A mosquito's birth dwarfs the gulf. Bickering affirms the universe. The mind is a region of redemption. The mouth wishes for a banana. Tap a fiber.

Is Heisenberg's Uncertainty Principle an observational problem or is it built into the structure of the universe?

It's been over a month now that Oriana received her orchids. They're doing well. They lean meaningfully into the sun.

Oriana goes for her morning walk and returns to tell me about the hole where Safeway used to be. It fascinates her. For the last several weeks we've been witness to an ongoing cavalcade of big trucks carrying loads of dirt down Taylor from the old Safeway, which is gone. There's now a huge gaping hole where the store formerly stood. The vividness of that store, after shopping there for so many years, is very much with us. The deli, the produce section with its fine mists, the dairy, the wine department, the meat department, the pharmacy – all of it gone. The new Safeway will be very different. It will be at the bottom of a 7-level residential building. This is the future. Confirmed by dirt. Load upon load of dirt. Where does it go? What will it be used for? In the end, dirt is everything. Everything worms. Everything corn. Everything oak. Everything elm and yew and buried under a stone. Everything. Everything needed for posts and barns and raising horses and vegetables and flowers. Everything root. Everything grave. Dirt.

I asked Proust, what are your feelings about dirt? There was no answer. Proust was not in the room. He was elsewhere, listening to a piece of music. The music, as he described it, created a sense of expectation which it sustained for a period of time, long enough to greet the next note and hold the door open to let it into the composition, where it crashed around in his heart like a wild animal, clawing at it and giving him exquisite pain. But, yes, he likes dirt.

I like being radical. Radical as in root: deep, fundamental, life-nourishing. And radical as in extreme. Intensity is intoxicating. I believe that's what is partly meant in AA by a "dry drunk."

The thing with intensity is this: it's a way to break through to the ultimate reality of things, break past appearances, gain ultimate freedom when the constraints of logic and rationality come crashing down. This is why rock'n'roll was such a threat back in the day. It promoted eccentricity, mania, madness, weirdness, Rabelaisian Polyphemes of macabre disorder. Where intensity truly excels is in the uninhibited pleasures of sex. It conveys transport. It spits on conventionality. It sneers at fatuous bourgeois comfort. It arches its back and rubs up against the leg of Charles Baudelaire. It purrs. It whines. It howls for attention. It terrorizes some; others it just pisses off. But when its charisma fuels the evangelist or rock star, people are magnetized by it. You can't cage it in consistency or coherence. Intensity excites the molecules of contrariety until it boils and rattles the lid and the teapot whistles and steam drips from the ceiling. Anyone with an appreciation of intoxication knows this. Intensity rips the door off its hinges. Intensity bends the bars of the jail and out walks a monster of incalculable strength. Eyes blood-red with vision.

If Frankenstein was about the abuses of science, the wolf-man movies were about the perversions to the spirit brought about by constraints of formality and good behavior. The asphyxiating hebetude of normality. The craven need for a sense of security, even if acquired through the humility of compliance. The bars that constrain our rage during a full moon are imaginary.

There's nothing in life that can't be solved with four hundred matches and a colonoscopy.

What's most difficult to render from one language into another is cadence.

Some things can't be said right away. They must be led up to, couched within a sandwich of nouns and prepositions, the charcuterie of conversation. Speech can be tricky. Writing allows for a little more expansion. Things can be thought out. A thousand nuances that hadn't been considered emerge in the play of light and shadow.

Green has never been one of my favorite colors. I don't know why I'm not fonder of it. It seems like a color that would naturally induce feelings of pleasure by its association with forests and alpine meadows, in the same way that blue induces feelings of transcendence by its association with the sky, or red induces feelings of heat and high passion. Green, a calm color, induces feelings of calm, which is nice, who doesn't want to feel calm? The fact is, though, calm can be dull. It's crisis and cataclysm that bring out a truly exciting luminescence within our being, even when it's mixed with fear, because fear is exciting, and so are anger and longing, these are all the hues of intensity, which is scarlet. White is frightening and possesses a strangely forbidding beauty because of its associations with ice and snow, with blank movie screens before the movie begins, with refrigerators and freezers and the décor of ice cream parlors. An exception might be *White Heat* with James Cagney and that final scene in which he screams "Top of the world, Ma! Top of the world!" Brown is as intellectual as Rembrandt. Yellow are daisies and sunflowers and butter and the giant blazing star that is the sun itself in all its glory. Black is the obstinacy of obsidian and the cold blank nothingness that is space. Green is sad. And behind it, the grin of Pan.

I must say I enjoy fantasizing about money and being rich. Not insanely rich, not Jeff Bezos rich, just rich enough to buy a house if a certain architectural style catches my fancy, or a yacht, or a library filled with ancient manuscripts and sculptures of the great authors and visionaries, at which point my balloon pops. Visionary and rich are incongruities. Incompatible. Maybe not so much in the so-called real world where it's possible a visionary could feasibly be rich. It's my private ethos that prevents my fantasy of wealth going beyond certain limits. And the fact that it is somewhere tethered inwardly to a principle I don't fully understand, or indeed how it got there, but it's there alright, gleaming like the world's largest diamond in an ultra-secure glass case protected by a web of red laser beams. It's wealth, of a sort, but not the sort of wealth I could use to pay for a *tartare de bœuf Normand taillé au couteau* at the Bouillon Racine in Paris, or a ticket to see Alison Krauss and Robert Plant on the Pyramid Stage at the Glastonbury Festival, all on a whim in a whirlwind of jet-set extravagance. It's the sort of wealth where I listen to Alison Krauss and Robert Plant on YouTube, and keep my ethics in a noumenal account, plump with variables.

Dwell is such a different word from inhabit. Imagine if Presley had sung I found a new place to inhabit rather than I found a new place to dwell. Dwelling is serious. Think of a house. Any house. You enter and smell a mingling of sweat, coffee and bacon, and clothes tossed over the back of the couch, and a cat in the window, and the TV on. Dwell means finding shelter in a world of granite men and savage schemes. Dragons with black membranous wings ribbed and feathered and broad and clawed. I dwell in the natural accidentals of a polyphonic music. This is my residence. Here I dwell. That's my last dinner on the wall. Spaghetti and meatballs. How did it get there? Don't ask. And over there is the shaggy face of my alter ego, drooped in rumination. The figure to the right is the ivory gear of a Lamborghini on the road to redemption, driven by a mutant being with zigzag tattoos and a big gold tooth. That would be uncle Ziggy on his way to Monaco. Ziggy doesn't dwell. He lives for the moment. Or rents it.

So much thick red hair, it looks like the Colorado River flowing out of her head and cascading down. Margo Timmons. Cowboy Junkies. "Sweet Jane," live performance.

It occurs to me that a hoe is an odd implement. Not like a rake. A rake is obvious. A hoe is a single blade, but for what? Pulling? Smoothing? It's not aggressive, like a rake. Certainly not a saw. Not a nail. Not a hammer. Not a planet. Just a hoe. A blank dull hoe leaning against the black velvet background of a painting abandoned and put in the garage with the gardening tools ... that will one afternoon be pounded into the dirt and pull up clods of earth teeming with worms. A bit like a pen. Pounded into paper and squiggled, behind it the description of itself in a cloud of butterflies. Reality is a tool we use to describe what happens when we see a lure put before our eyes in a dark, voluptuous, somewhat cheesy room where drinks are served on the lips of fate.

Is it possible to be carefully careless or carelessly careful at all the appropriate times and lead a healthy and prosperous life? What would it take to sing like Etta James? No one knows the value of time like a dishwasher. Maybe a pilot. Maybe a scuba diver who works professionally on salvaging crews. They know the value of time. They know it gives, takes, devours and produces all simultaneously, and that this happens in space, which enters by climbing the mountain and exits with a row of camels silhouetted against the sky. They know the slow shadow of their hidden life shows signs of mending. That the bold pass quickly from patience to annoyance. That clocks are dry but pomegranates are juicy. And blue women are a sign of trouble in a time of heaven. And green men play orange drums on the dunes of Mauritania.

I miss the Midwest, but not the mosquitos. I miss the dirt and tractors, the weight of the sky buttressed against a horizon of crosses and signs. Form is Monday. The pen is a claw that feels its way toward dying. It isn't long before the substitutes become institutes. I wish the land would return to being a vast expanse of grass and wind and buffalo. And it will. One day. Not today. Today is pants and shoes and glass. Bones and rice deepen my respect for lightning. The window awakens as the moon undresses. A sumptuous Tuesday of stars and grass arrives on a little noble axle with two wheels and a daring summer rhapsody of bees and soap. Saturday laughs upstairs. Sunday sits and sews fragments of Wednesday on a Thursday chair upholstered with Friday's climate of time ticking out tickets of wind at the door. And a cuckoo pops out. It's the face of Groucho Marx, with a big grin, big cigar, thick funny greasepaint eyebrows, and all the time in the world.

July 15th, 2022, Mick Jagger sings "Wild Horses" to a crowd in Vienna. He wears an unbuttoned purple silk shirt, black pants, black T-shirt, and is as skinny as hell. Quick and supple. From the neck down, he could be 18. But the face is deeply wrinkled. The crags of a life lived in ways I can only speculate, but certainly with flair and intensity. As for those horses, they're still wild. One would have to confess there's a definite defiance of age going on. The energy it takes to keep stoking those fires must be enormous. Very taxing. But it can be done. Apparently. In Vienna. Where Mozart gave piano lessons. And Anton Webern led the Vienna Workers' Chorus. Skinny 79-year-old Englishman singing "Honky Tonk Women" in spry éclats of jubilant energy, and it makes you laugh to think the inevitable deteriorations of age can be fobbed off like that, and in Vienna, in a shiny purple shirt.

Incendies en Gironde. I watch the wildfires in France on the French news. *Le journal de France 2 vingt heures.* The scene is terrifying. Huge devouring flames destroying thousands of acres of forest in a country scorched by drought and heatwave. Thousands of people evacuated from homes and camping grounds. The situation is even worse in Spain and Portugal. Here in the U.S. 36,877 wildfires so far this year have burned 5,238,977 acres of forest.

A fiery image on the front of Croatian newspaper *24sata* shows the usually sylvan Dalmatian coast with the stark headline: "Hell."

It's a daily preoccupation. How to process this reality. This catastrophic drama occurring every day now. It's so huge. Apocalyptic. Hard to take it all in. At home, life still has most of the features of normalcy intact. We continue to enjoy that luxury. It's when we go somewhere by car that we see all the homeless encampments, boarded-up businesses, graffiti everywhere, all the streets in disrepair, despairing faces behind the wheel, shootings due to road rage on the rise. "We think in generalities, but we live in detail," said Alfred North Whitehead.

Triggers, bullets, mendacity. Conceits, illusions, urns.

A young woman in a thong energetically pumping an inflatable paddleboard on the hot asphalt of a Seattle parking lot.

A stove in an abandoned house near Anaconda, Montana that still works, though nobody can explain where the electricity is coming from. A magpie on a barbed wire fence jiggles an old wooden post as it takes off.

In the National Gallery, London, there hangs a portrait of an unknown woman painted by an unknown artist around 1470. She wears an elaborate headpiece of white fabric, spotless and pristine, upon which reposes a housefly, rendered in such detail you can make out the shadow of its body. Why? Why did the artist include a housefly on an otherwise immaculate headpiece? The lady, who wears a slight smile, must have been in on the joke. And here it is, 552 years later, and everyone's first reaction is to swat that nasty fly away so we can see the art, realizing a bit later that the fly is as much a part of the art as the delicacy of the woman's eyelashes and her beautiful soft skin and the brocade of her dress.

Oriana goes for a short walk after dinner and returns to tell me that the tree we marveled at the other day for its huge pear-shaped leaves and beautiful white flowers is a southern catalpa. She has another app that identities trees and shrubs. I wonder what would come up if you took a picture of Robert Plant's head of hair. Would it be identified as a Muskogee Squeegee or a Blonde Dalliance (Now Going Gray)? I think it's either an Apache Plume or Toadflax.

I once asked Jimmy Page how long it took him to grow his hair. He was sitting in the back seat of a limousine with the other members of The Yardbirds and had just finished a performance at the San Carlos Auditorium in San José, California. He was young, at 22 only four years older than me, but already an old hand at the guitar. He treated it like an appendage, an outgrowth so integral to his being it had the power of a white metallic prosthetic for fountaining fire and shooting bolts of lightning into the audience. I'd just been forced to get a haircut because back then (1966) long hair would prevent you from getting any kind of job. Just walking down the street was an invitation for insults and sneers. I was very upset. I felt very unnatural without my hair, like Samson after Delilah snipped his locks. Two months, said Page. I bought him a Coke.

Lucinda Williams likes doing a J.J. Cale song called "Magnolia." It's extraordinarily beautiful. Her voice has the lilt of the southwest in it, the perfume of a Tucson sunset. "Whippoorwill singing / soft summer breeze / Makes me think of my babe / I left down in New Orleans."

I've never been to New Orleans. It has long occupied a place in my imagination. I've often thought of visiting there. It was painful, in August 2005, to see the devastation caused by hurricane Katrina, and shocking to witness the neglect of the U.S. government while people clambered onto rooftops, waving shirts and rags, hoping to be picked up by a helicopter. About 16,000 people, mostly black, were jammed into the Superdome, where a 2-year-old girl slept in a pool of urine, the air conditioning failed, a swampy heat filled the dome, and the lights went off. There was no sanitation. Faeces absolutely everywhere, including the walls. The dome was patrolled by 500 Louisiana National Guard carrying machine guns, as people pressed against metal barricades pleading for water and help.

New Orleans is considered by many to be the most European city in the U.S. I can see that, a little, but to my mind it's the most indefinable. How do you characterize a place known for its gumbo and Voodoo, jazz funerals and Mardi Gras? African cultures were hugely influential, chiefly West Africa and the Congo River basin. New Orleans is said to be the birthplace of jazz, one of the greatest artistic developments in the 20th century. Louis Armstrong, Jelly Roll Morton, Pete Fountain, Trombone Shorty. Fats Domino, Irma Thomas, Aaron Neville. "Tell it Like it Is."

Lately, I've been thinking about origins. The origins of language. The origins of art. The origins of sugar. The origins of the weekend. The origins of film. The origins of photography. The origins of origami. The origins of the ostrich. And pharmacies and farms and the whole idea of ownership and property. Who first got it into their head that they owned an expanse of dirt? Ostensibly arable dirt. For growing wheat or yams or rice or corn. And owned a house and cattle and goats and trees and water and the labor of people. How do you own these things? What does it mean to own these things? Isn't ownership just an illusion? It's impossible to own anything. What you're really doing by claiming you own something is to stop other people from using it. And so owning something, anything, an iron mine, diamond mine, silverware, dishware, hardware, glassware, healthcare is to exclude and control and lose your humanity and become a reptilian thing huddled in a corner counting cryptocurrency in the eerie white glow of a computer. And the fear of losing it causes an obsession to acquire more and more and more, and the more you own the more you fear losing it, until it becomes a mania that owns you hook line and sinker.

I find it amusing that the YouTube algorithms have put Spanish violinist Lina Tur Bonet and her rendition of Beethoven's *Sonata per uno mulaticco lunattico* in a mix of blues songs including three different versions of Elmore

James' "It Hurts Me Too" (one by Eric Clapton, one by Jeremy Spencer, and one by Luther Allison) and Howlin' Wolf and Albert King and John Mayall and Stevie Ray Vaughn and Muddy Waters and Jimi Hendrix, and yet it fits in there fine, there's nothing incongruous about it whatever. It's a crazy piece of music, the notes are all over the musical map, some of them frenzied some of them breezy some of them so high-pitched and hurly-burly they're more like fire than music, and then it gets real quiet and sad and whammo it explodes again into all kinds of fireworks and plucked strings and eerie vibrato.

I haven't yet mentioned my spaceship. The work is going well. I'm in a bit of a panic to get going. Elon Musk has the right idea. This planet is doomed. Should be obvious. So here it is: a tall gleaming cylinder of magical alloys I cooked up in the splendor of my basement laboratory and assembled piece by piece using nothing but words and the nacreous linings of shellfish. Phosphorous digits that will glow on the control panel and keep us hopeful in the fearful reaches of cold dark space as we leave the solar system and head out towards the exo-planet of our choice. It will be fueled by imagination and paper and the flip side of despair with all of its eudaimonic potential and crazy electrons. More specifically, it will be a mixture of decaying algae, the belch of a walrus, the moan of a sunset dropped on the toe of morning, a box of God particles, 200 drops of dimethyl-tryptamine, and the propulsive charm of a Reykjavik back-rub.

Just recently, in several letters between friends, the idea of intelligences other than human on planet Earth popped up. It seems to be on people's minds lately. But yes, I agree, and would go further, and say the entire universe is suffused with intelligence. It's so obvious. The harmony and consistency of physical laws coupled with the discordancy and inconsistencies of the subatomic realm, and how these things interact to create phenomena of spectacular ingenuity, imply a vigorous and inventive cognition. Chaos is vital to the overall harmony of the universe, and to the peculiar manifestations of each planet. The evolution of life on Earth, from one-celled prokaryotic bacterium that lived some 3 billion years ago to the spread of fingers now dancing on a computer keyboard to write these words, and the infinite diversity of creatures that adapt to challenging and ever-changing environments thanks to the exquisite workings of natural selection, exhibits abundant evidence that everything is driven by some underlying intelligence.

I go remove the laundry from the washing machine and put it in the dryer. I like to spin the aluminum drum of the washing machine to see if anything is sticking to the upper part of the drum where I'm unable to see anything, an errant sock or fugitive washcloth. It amazes me that we have machines to wash clothes. We have, in our bedroom, a painting by Van Gogh of some washerwomen washing clothes in a canal under a drawbridge (specifically, The Langlois Bridge, which was replaced with a concrete bridge in 1930, and then blown up by retreating Germans during WWII). The women are hunched together in full, roundish shapes of strong primary color. They seem stocky because of the heaviness of their clothing, which heightens the feeling of labor and camaraderie. My dad got the print for me when he and my stepmother were visiting the Van Gogh Museum in Amsterdam. It's a print, of course, not the actual painting.

My parents were fond of giving me items pertaining to Van Gogh. I was the Van Gogh of the family, the eccentric artist who would always be struggling to make art in dire poverty. Proof, I suppose, of a tacit approval of some kind. Though I never did care for Puccini's opera *La Bohème* and the way it glamourizes the poverty of the artists, which has long been the secret fantasy of the bourgeoisie, and for which they pat themselves on the back for having avoided despite the interminable and spiritless tedium of their lives. I think it's a fair exchange. There's absolutely nothing glamorous or romantic about poverty. Believe me, I'm an expert in this field.

I remember the day I spent looking for Van Gogh's bridge in Arles. Didn't find it. Didn't realize, at the time, that the bridge no longer existed. I found something instead, a gypsy festival at Saintes-Maries-de-la-Mer, and Jerry Hopkins, author of *No One Here Gets Out Alive*, a biography of Jim Morrison. We had dinner and exchanged postcards for a few years.

You don't hear the word "brine" much anymore, although, it has to said, I don't remember a time when it was commonly in use. If we say the sea is salty, we say the sea is salty, not full of brine or tinctured with brine or brindled with brine or bright with brine or shot like a bolt of lightning from a bow of brine. And I wonder if there are people who make it their mission, their calling, to go around using words that no one uses anymore. People gifted with invention who know how to get a conversation going and guide it toward places where that word might fit into the colloquy in a manner that makes it seem natural and not shoehorned in to put the word on display. Like I just did with the word colloquy. Nothing ruins a conversation like ostentation. Except poker. Then it's all about eyes. All about attitude and disguise. This is a different kind of language, a vocabulary of looks and facial expressions, sly glances, hidden calculations, the careful reading of a misleading sign. It's cold and dark like the water under a dock. The look of lurk. The slither of camouflage.

Sooner or later I must exempt myself from the adventure of meaning and find something different to talk about, something embryonic and irascible, something electric, something slippery, something kaleidoscopic and thrilling, something thriving like a throat but thin like a lip, hollow like the jaw of a maudlin mandolin. If the sassafras ruptures, if the earthquake arrives, if the hurricane sits down at the dinner table with a wink and a negligee, if the monsoon should win at tennis with a strong forearm and a periodical regret, then the tiller in the field will be perpendicular to the funicular, and the particular will be lenticular, singular as the scimitar for sale in Singapore, which comes with an altimeter, a calligrapher, and a bottle of vinegar.

I envy artists. Visual artists. Painters. The sensuality of paint. The sexuality of paint. Smearing paint on a canvas with a brush is muscular, blithely physical, and fun. I can see the great satisfaction in molding space, slathering colors, making symphonies of phthalo green, snaking reds and yellows loud as suns. Working with words obliges one to employ a different species of attention. It's a different kind of focus. You feel the weight of semantic verdure, the push toward verisimilitude, while – if one is poetically inclined – the fight against interpretation, against reification and symbol, against artificial limits and the asphyxiating weight of tendentious virtue-signaling, the underlying expectation of arriving at great insights, great wisdom and rear admirals dispensing orders in the smoke of battle. There's the continual search for the exhilaration of music. Words set free, even from the cage of music, the symmetries of rhythm and confinement of solfege, the tensions and resolutions of notes rendered edgy by a backbeat. So that unconscious forces can rise from their repression and bend the bars and escape into the cool night air, spread its wings and rise against the stars silhouetted against a full moon.

So what am I espousing? I don't know what I'm espousing. I just worry about the world. The world is on fire. On fire with fire. Literal fire. Metaphorical fire, too. The burning words of the backward, the smoldering words of the resentful, the blazing words of malcontent poets, the invisible nobility of the rebellious hurling Molotov cocktails at invisible empires of hegemonic greed and garbage propaganda, the nitroglycerin of streetcar wizards riding the ghostly rails of a failed culture, the midnight journeys of propane pirates, the phosphorous glow of buffalo bones in the Rockies, the thunderous explosions of Stratocaster transmissions in the engine of night.

My shirt felt damp, putting it on a moment ago. I must've sweated more than I thought while going up those steep steps on the south side of Queen Anne Hill. It was warm – 80 degrees or so, a delicious sensation – on a late afternoon in mid-July. Oriana and I had had dinner with two friends at a casual brewpub called Brodie's Beer & Hopopolis. It was the first face-to-face conversation we'd had with anyone other than ourselves in months. We'd become almost more accustomed to seeing people on Zoom or Skype, their faces pixelating in and out on a small laptop screen. It's so much nicer having a conversation with real people. They were in a celebratory mood on account of Oriana's recent retirement. They were genuinely glad for her. They're warm people, a few years younger than Oriana and I, and have a way of making you feel relaxed. I was able to let loose with some of my political views, many of which had become unpopular as they had to do with my thoughts on the Covid vaccines, especially after listening to Mike Tyson interview Robert F. Kennedy, Jr on a video podcast. Our friends were tolerant of my views, and judging by their silence I suspect they disagreed with some aspects of it, but these were open-minded people, a near-extinct species these days. I also spoke to them about Mike Tyson and how I admired him.

He's a good interviewer, asking pertinent questions and not interrupting. His overall demeanor is calm and he speaks in a disarming, soft-spoken voice. This reminded me of a newsletter I'd received that morning from the French Philosophy magazine to which I subscribe. The letter was written by a woman – I'm assuming somewhat young – and was about how she'd been benefiting from boxing lessons. One of the first lessons had been a little paradoxical: boxing is not about fighting. Boxing is an art. It stimulates the mind as much as the body. Jack Dempsey used to memorize whole plays by Shakespeare before entering the ring. It focused his mind. It gave him rhythm and balance. And what is writing but a form of shadow boxing?

We talked about climate change and all the raging wildfires in the world. Melting glaciers, rising seas, crop failures, and rivers running dry. Lake Mead and Lake Powell are about to become sandboxes. A farmer in France scoops up a handful of dust where he'd planted wheat. He was standing in a field of what appeared to be dead brittle grass. *Le blé devrait être jusqu'ici,* he said, pointing to his thigh. "The wheat should be this high." The dry, brittle, strawlike growth beneath him rose only to ankle height. And I thought of the medieval hunger rocks that began appearing when the rivers of Europe shrank to record lows. I thought about David Bowie's song "Five Years" which – though it first appeared 50 years ago on the 1972 album *The Rise and Fall of Ziggy Stardust and the Spiders from Mars* – is now terrifyingly pertinent. "Pushing through the market square / So many mothers sighing (sighing) / News had just come over / We had five years left to cry in." We changed the subject.

They had just seen the comic Maria Bamford. I love Maria Bamford. Big fan. I have a huge appetite for the eccentric, weirdness a tad macabre, or a lot macabre, gallows humor, and the voice she impersonates so beautifully of a confident, well-adjusted woman who feels in control of her life and is eternally convinced of a bright and fulfilling future, and the falseness of it, and the sad artificiality of its cheerfulness, the tragicomical cherry nucleating its chocolate sphere.

It's always nice to return home. That's when I took off my shirt and shoes and got a book from the shelf, *Concrete* by Thomas Bernhard. I added a bottle of water, some Tums, and my earphones and laptop to the mix and adjusted some pillows and lay down on the bed. Reading is always a transformative experience, especially when you've got the time to really immerse yourself in some writing, and quite frequently, after I've read a paragraph or two, I get my own stream of words going. They float by like chyrons on a news show, semantic trinkets telegramming catastrophes of phosphorescent whatness. Can I get a witness? Can I get a bath? Can I get ahead? Can I can I can I? Let me open a door to your brain & do it in segments. I have the unmitigated sadness of the cargo barge. It's all pasta and past the hope of tenderloin. I'm a pendulum of perfume in a planetarium made of harpsichord knots and ingots of hot gold love.

I rarely think of myself as Elvis Presley. Actually, to be perfectly frank, I never think of myself as Elvis Presley. I've got the ego for it, and sneer, but not the gold lamé. No black hair with a pompadour and a ducktail. No limousine. No ability to play the guitar. Or sing. I'm more of a Philip Whalen kind of guy. Or Ted Berrigan. Or Matsuo Basho. I like quiet moments. Orchids and frogs. The waves in the brown stained oak of my writing desk, which seem to pulse to the south, drift to the north, then slowly rotate like the Indian Ocean Gyre. I'm drawn magnetically to Whalen's marvelous distillates and observations, how the back of the chair bends outwards as well as up, a wraith of feathery clouds between moon and ocean, Klein's bottle made from varicolored glass, Kirttimukha, the Face of Glory, a walking stick insect in white cotton batting, two pigeons in sunlight, broken glass, tin cans, weeds and squirrels, and you who are the Buddhas of this world.

I watch a YouTube video of Indochine, a Parisian rock group, sing "*Un été français*" atop La Grande Arche de la Défense, a big production with fireworks shooting out and Paris in the background, hardly visible at night but for the twinkling of its lights. They evince a certain French energy, indefinable but vivid, you know it when you see it, the fire in Rimbaud's eyes, even in those photos he took of himself, which didn't come out very well, those wet plate negatives were hard to deal with and required a great deal of water, which was probably somewhat scarce in Harar. The water he used was filthy, avers Lucille Pennel, curator of an exhibit of Rimbaud's photographs for the Arthur Rimbaud Museum in Charleville-Mézières. The images will eventually fade. My favorite is the old man in the marketplace amid ancient stone columns.

Ice cream isn't toes. I've been thinking about this all day. How the tornadoes whirl around in my bones. How the trumpets of heaven blast through the sky. How the fat booms of the chloroform sperm wiggle by in the ethereal serum of everything holy and wet and honest and wild. How I found Philip Whalen's mind on page 175 hopping up and down in a sequined hallelujah. Would snapdragons be facetious in a cemetery? The answer is somewhere south of life. If you squeeze a word long enough it will squirt the gold of cognition into your mind. Your thoughts will float on silver rivers full of serendipitous shallows. Rainbow trout. And Philip Whalen in an inner tube.

I change the bulbs in the bedside lamp. It's shaped like a candelabra, and silver. In color, anyway. It's probably a metal alloy that resembles silver. The bulbs were cold to the hand and felt like glass breasts while I screwed and lifted them out of their respective sockets. The new bulbs are energy-saving bulbs. The old incandescent bulbs are completely gone now. I generally don't like energy-saving bulbs as they're never bright enough and there's often something dreary about the light they cast. But these bulbs are pretty good. They put out a nice bright light.

Oriana draws a nuthatch. We hear robins outside our kitchen window. They're out there every night, shortly after the sun has dipped beneath the horizon. Why do they wait so long to sing? We guess because it's quiet. They can hear themselves. They can communicate. They sing in the early morning, too, when the first light of dawn shoots above the ridges of the Cascades to the east.

I wonder what happened to that cigar thing that drifted through our solar system in 2017. Scientists named it Oumuamua, a Hawaiian word meaning "a messenger from afar arriving first." It wasn't a comet. Comets have comas, the trail of dust and gas that trails behind a comet. The highly elongated object was identified, speculatively, as being an asteroid. It had a dark red color, a degree of brightness at least 10 times more reflective than our solar system's typical space rocks – shiny enough to suggest the gleam of burnished metal – and it demonstrated an unexpected boost in speed which some scientists attributed to jets of gaseous material from its surface. Unusual variations in the object's brightness suggested that it was rotating on more than one axis. Harvard astronomer Avi Loeb declared that the object was sent by aliens and might be a form of "light sail" spacecraft. The reaction from his peers in astronomy was resoundingly hostile. They called his speculation sensationalist and ill-motivated. Loeb's theory skyrocketed him into celebrity status. He fought back, arguing that the search for alien life was grossly underfunded and that more money was spent on studying gravity waves, something that has little impact on society. I don't know what to make of any of this. I personally gravitate more toward Oumuamua being an alien ship. Perhaps, avers Loeb, in a time when Earth faces an urgent global warming crisis, it could be finding extraterrestrial life that saves us from ourselves. Well, yeah. But I wouldn't hold my breath. Has anyone suggested that Oumuamua might actually have been a cigar? Imagine Goya's Saturn puffing away in Orion's horsehead nebula with a satisfied look after dining on his progeny. Or it might've been a giant candy bar, Milky Way or Mars Bar.

We keep a black hole in our closet. We're in love with its naked singularities. There's a voice coming out of it. It sounds like clothes. It's got that combination of comfort and pretense. Tender buttons. Clever zippers. And the velvet warmth I feel when I slide my hand and arm into the black hole. I don't know why we keep it in there. It doesn't look great under the coffee table. Or the bed. And anyway, I don't like sleeping over a black hole; it makes me nervous. We prefer it in the closet. The closet was invented for things like that. Everything about it is inversely proportional to the familiar comforts of the living room. It's why we like it. It's good to have something in the house that eludes any possibility of tedium. The French don't have closets, they have armoires. Not the same thing. Armoires are furniture. Closets are rooms. They're places you can go inside, if it's not too cluttered, and feel the interactions between collars and sleeves, gravity and space, and my array of spectral ties, especially the black one, which is a ribbon of reverie sucking in everything.

Oriana shows me a photograph of Eudora Welty's house in Alabama. It's a nice little house. The bedroom is cozy and quite tidy. The dirt outside the house is red. Oriana asks what makes the dirt red. Iron, I say. Iron oxides. There's a good supply of oxygen in the subsoil. It's well drained. Must be all that humidity. What's the difference between dirt and clay? she asks. You mean what makes clay clay? I don't know what makes clay clay. Turns out it's the size of the particles. Clay is defined as any mineral inorganic substance that is smaller than 0.002mm, whereas particles of silt can range in size from .002 to .06mm. I like silt. But not as much as walking in sand. That white sand by Carmel is really sweet under the feet. And I still remember that lone guitarist sitting out there on a foggy summer day in Carmel in 1965. The Beatles midway into their career. The Stones, too, when they were raw and a bit sleazy and brash and cheeky and who would stay together as a band – minus Brian Jones and Charlie Watts (deceased), and Bill Wyman, who's retired from the group and busy finding Roman and Celtic coins with a metal detector – until now, and still going strong. I tell Oriana that Lucinda Williams came out with a tribute album to the Rolling Stones. She's got the right voice. Soulful, seasoned, gritty. Full of beautiful imperfections. And red clay.

On our way home from a short run around the top of Queen Anne on a Saturday afternoon in late July, we enter Bhy Kracke park just as three men on bicycles appear, all of them shouting loudly. Their shouts are subverbal and hurt the ears. "Men of refinement," I say. Oriana urges me to be quiet. I tell her this outpouring of manly bravado is all show. If I made a fist they'd tuck their tails and run, happy to avoid a testosterone-induced imbroglio with a geriatric weirdo. Just previous to our entering the little switchback trail that takes us to the bottom, the cyclists go down the path shouting loudly, mostly to avoid colliding with the pedestrians walking on the trail, most of whom appear irritated. I don't blame them. Oriana tells me she wants to show me something. She leads me to a small section of the park walled in by trees and a number of immense rhododendrons, most of which are dead. This is what she wanted to show me. There were a few new branches and leaves growing out of the trunk. She found this rather astonishing, that something this dead still had enough life in it to make another attempt at putting out leaves and maybe some flowers. The rhododendron has a long and storied past. The nectar of some species of rhododendron was used to make a hallucinogenic beverage the Romans were fond of. They called it "mad honey." It originated in the Black Sea region of Eastern Turkey, where bees pollinate fields of rhododendron flowers which produce a neurotoxin called grayanotoxin which, when consumed, can cause light-headedness, feelings of euphoria and hallucinations. Too much can lead to vomiting and diarrhea. In 67 B.C.E. in Trabzon, a city on the northeast coast of Turkey, Gnaeus Pompeius Magnus (Pompey the Great) and his Roman army were chasing King Mithridates of Pontus and his Persian army along the Black Sea. The Persians gathered pots of local honey and left them for the Roman troops to find. And find them they did. They ate the honey and became disoriented. The Persian army returned and killed over 1,000 of the Romans with few losses of their own. It occurs to me to make some mad honey and hand jars of it out to loud cyclists.

We get to the door of our condo building and Oriana undoes the flap on her fanny pack where she keeps peanuts for the crows. The Velcro is amazingly loud. "You wouldn't want that on a commando raid," I tell her. The invention of Velcro was inspired by the burdock root. A Swiss inventor named George de Mestral applied himself to removing burs from his dog's fur. Curious about how firmly the burs clung to the fur, he put some under a microscope and saw that the burs were hooked. Velcro soon followed. The burdock root also reputedly has some medicinal qualities and has long been used to make tinctures, elixirs, ointments and teas.

"A work is never completed," remarked Paul Valery, "except by some accident such as weariness, satisfaction, the need to deliver, or death: for, in relation to who or what is making it, it can only be one stage in a series of inner transformations." It's the "series of inner transformations" part that arouses my interest. That feels right. That feels like what's happening each immeasurable moment. Each instant. Each altered attitude. Each epiphany, minor, major, or multifarious. Each memorable meal. Each step that takes me further into a foreign country, or understanding, which is a Polynesia of the mind, an archipelago of oceanic consciousness. Each tremor in the blood. Each time I feel the exhilaration of words in ecstatic gestation. Each lift of the seesaw. Each descent of the seesaw. Each time I see a seesaw I seize the fulcrum of the moment to Chippewa each squeak of my walking shoes. The black fabric of the ones I wore in Paris turned powdery yellow from the ubiquitous limestone. Each day I do what I need to do, I feel the morning wander into the fullness of the afternoon. Each time I don't I gloat. Each night I go to bed and lose consciousness, and I marvel at how this happens every day, this little taste of death, this lovely dissolve. Each time I change my mind I find a lemon in my lime. Each time I take a deep breath and go into society to be sociable, I discover that it's all theatre, which is fine, but nobody gave me my lines. Each time I get a parking ticket I delight in not paying it, at least for a minute or two. Each time I'm greeted by a cat and a wife and a warm room, I insist that this is bliss. Each time I play a song on YouTube and it triggers a rapture of all the things I'm able to grab and let go and let my head get empty and feel my bones settle into the warmth of my blood as dotted crotchets pulse through my arms and legs open to the universe.

"What's this?" I ask Oriana. There's a small vial on the kitchen windowsill with a bit of pale yellowish goo at the bottom. "It's water," she says. "It's good to soak tomato seeds before planting them. It helps them to germinate. It softens the seeds." Oriana has been growing baby tomatoes for several months now. The plants are amazingly tall. They sit, potted, at the far edge of the driveway at the front of our building.

Oriana has become a fan of Vandana Shiva, physicist, environmental activist and author. "Seed is created to renew, to multiply, to be shared, and to spread," she says. "Seed is life itself." Ms Shiva maintains a strong oppositional stance against corporations such as Monsanto, who have converted seed to private property and attempt to have total control over it. She describes attempts by U.S. companies and organizations to patent Indian plants such as neem, basmati rice, and paigamabari, an ancient wheat variety. "This is piracy from nature and cultures that preserve knowledge," she declaims. "Seed is not an invention."

Make life less complicated. So says an ad for Volvo. Beneath the blurb is a photo of a young man working on a car in a garage. He's bending over the engine and has a tool in his hand. I take note of how well-groomed he is. His hair is parted and his beard is trimmed. He looks more like a college professor or surgeon than a mechanic. But it's true: why spend hours on YouTube or some other tutorial trying to get a handle on how to fix your car yourself when you could bring it to a professional mechanic who would apply a skillset that took years of experience to acquire and do a far better job on your car while you pursue interests you find more fruitful and enjoyable? A seasoned individual knows when to delegate. Life in the 21st century is absurdly complex, thanks to a technocracy that explodes with innovations every minute of the day, innovations that do more to complicate life than to increase efficiency or ease of use.

I remember needing to change the water pump on a 1965

Dodge Dart and taking it to a local garage where they told me (I was young and a bit bedraggled, the impoverished scholar look) the pump is easy to change and I would save a considerable amount of money if I did it myself. They meant well, but the time and labor of attempting to fix it myself was herculean. I spent an entire day under the chassis. I was living in a boarding house at the time, and one of the tenants, seeing my misery, came to my aid and with the aid of a socket wrench helped me replace the pump. Never again, I told myself in solemn privacy. That's when I learned that I live in a culture with a mania for do-it-yourself solutions. Whether it's electrical, plumbing, drywall, car repair, constructing a small house in one's backyard or laying new tile in a kitchen or bathroom, people are evangelical about doing it themselves. It's as if there were some hidden agenda fueling the phenomenon, that strain, perhaps, of extreme individuality so exalted in our society. Prime example: John Wayne leaving the wagon train in John Ford's *Red River*, much against the pleading of the wagon-train members, including his betrothed love interest, who is killed in an Indian attack with the other members of the wagon train. Years later, John Wayne's tyrannical leadership causes the drovers to mutiny, and he shoots three of them. The movie dramatizes the conflict between the collective and the individual. This tension is inevitable in any society. Everyone resolves the problem in their own manner. I chose hiring the skilled, when I could afford it. As a result, I've acquired very few life skills but have grown a huge library, and prefer the treasures of the contemplative life over the mania for self-reliance. My self-esteem has never been hurt by hiring a plumber or electrician. I do, however, own a toolbox, just in case I'm forced by circumstances to invoke the spirit of self-reliance, a stubborn god that must be blandished with a look of determination and a monkey wrench in one hand.

"Shit Happens." It reads like a two-word novel. It encompasses all of life. The Buddha could've said it. Jesus could've said it. Mohammed, Maimonides, Martin Luther King and Thich Nhat Hahn could've said it. It could be a religion. You could call its devotees Shitites. And their head priest could wear an elaborate headpiece with the motto of their faith emblazoned on it in golden letters, and in Latin, *Defectio*. There's no analysis or hadron collider in the world that could break that phrase down into discrete, logical particles. Is the universe rational? It is not. The universe was born inherently chaotic. A chaotic system does not settle into a predictable pattern. Non-linear interactions between dark energy, dark matter, penguins and beer are clear indications that the universe cannot make up its mind about what it wants to be. Wrap your arms around it and try squeezing it. Output is not proportional to input. This is where intuition comes in: it somehow knows that Schrödinger's cat is both dead and alive. Intuition operates by mystical ingenuity. It eschews logic, and blithely understands the most basic tenet of life: shit happens.

I always liked that word, "liquidate" – to pay off, dispose of. It's quick on the tongue, that dental consonant at "date" is enameled and hard. The word is so sure of itself, so sure of what it's doing, of acquitting itself. You can let it slip and slide it around in your mouth all day. Occasions to use it are rare, however, unless you're a lawyer or banker. Not sure why I thought of it. Just one of those words that rises to the surface of the mind and bobs up and down in mesmerizing strangeness. What is liquid about liquidation? When substance turns liquid it gurgles, spirals down a drain.

Oriana repotted her orchid tonight. There were pretty yellow blooms on it, high stems and broad leaves, but no roots in dirt, since the orchid is an epiphyte, a plant that grows on another plant, but not parasitically, symbiotically, in a manner mutually beneficial to both. The seductive orchids draw the bees necessary for pollination. It's natural to think of them as feminine, but orchid is the Greek word for "testicle" because of the shape of the root tubers in some species of the genus Orchis. Oriana said the roots were packed in moss. She watched a bunch of tutorials on YouTube. She waited for the blooms to wither before unsettling the plant. Orchids are so frail. I hope the operation went well and there will be no complications. Everything in life feels so tentative, as if everything were on loan. Some things require payment, some don't – but which? Which don't? I don't know. I don't think there are paywalls in life. Or maybe they're there but I just don't see them most of the time. Lately I've been getting notifications that my subscription to life is nearly up. I can see it with my third eye.

I got the gardening bug late in life. I've always liked gardens, and I like most bugs, but I never got the urge to plant seeds, tend to the dirt, the needs and worms and percolations of dirt, do the weeding, the interminable weeding. My baptism to gardening was enforced. We were obligated as kids to do yard work. I think it had more to do with purification of the spirit, learning the Protestant work ethic etc. than learning the miracles and subtleties of sessile life. I'm sure that was intended as well, though held in silence, gardening being a practice that can't be inculcated too aggressively, like all things sacred and green, without risk of spoliation. Our tasks were never particularly challenging, I just never fully understood the instructions. I nodded, wanting to understand, but my state of irresolution lacked the enthusiasm to allow it to germinate. The bulk of my attention was spent standing, musing, leaning on a shovel in the rain.

What turned my mind was the suicide tree. The tree is subversive. It runs counter to all the tenets of capitalism and especially neo-liberal economics. The suicide tree, *Tachigalia versicolor*, is monocarpic: when it reaches maturity then dies within a year of that, it releases and disperses its seeds all around to a distance of up to 500 meters. This is a tree that can reach a height of 30 meters, produce one of the densest hardwoods in the old growth forests of Costa Rica and Columbia, then, when it falls and starts to decompose, leaves a large open space in the tree canopy for the sunlight to come through and nourish the seedlings on the forest floor. The tree is the opposite of competitive, the flourishing antithesis to the exaltation of ownership and tightfisted individuality that is virtually a religion in the industrialized world. It is self-sacrificial. It is an antipode to the billionaires, the techno-evangelists, the singulartarians. The essence of this tree has nothing to do with domination, competition or control. It doesn't exist to maximize its being over other beings. It exists to perish, and is interstitial, an entity of intervals and interludes and lulls. A symphony. But what's happening here, really? Is this just the intoxication of words, an instance of language obscuring rather than revealing reality? I don't think so. I sense something here that feels quite real. Goethe coined a word – *Urphänomen* – which referred to a phenomenon that is real (experienced) and ideal (conceptualized). I need to trust in my intuition more. The obsessive focus on principles of scientific objectivity unrelated to our subjectivity is wrong. It severs consciousness from the great loom of creation, the weave of interactions that result in electrons and kangaroos, the grammar of stars and the syntax of space, or the fall, one quiet afternoon, of a suicide tree.

Can one talk about the mind of plants as independent from one's own mind or the mind of others? Does ayahuasca talk to us when we're under its influence? And what is a mind? Maybe it's a water drop suspended at the flowery tip of a Banisteriopsis vine gathering the morning light. I once chewed a packet of Heavenly Blue Morning Glory seeds and it filled me with the warmest sense of well-being and outward affection for things that I'd ever felt. Was that the DNA of the morning glory communing with my DNA? Was it a form of chemical language? Is "chemical" the right word? Is the vocabulary of the morning glory rampant with preternatural graffiti? Consciousness might not be leaves or wind but the confluence of leaves and wind. Everything combined creates a symbiotic consciousness that is never one thing but all things. That's why it's so amusing to see things melt. One thing fuses with another thing to create a third thing. And a fourth thing and a fifth thing, and so on. I'm going to write a letter to a redwood in Humboldt County. I'm going to write it on the air. Stick it in a dandelion and blow it south.

When I'm feeling subjective I like to transfer tills and make up prices. I like to wax solipsistic and say things nobody understands except, perhaps, the dead. I like to make nets out of consonants and blow vowels of glass and view feelings from different points thanks to the parallax of syntax. Nobody is ever alone in a language. I mean, there's you, and then there's the language. You're in it up to your cerebral cortex. The only way out is by opening a word. And the only way in is by opening your mouth. The sherry is shiny and the gruel is unusual. The table is ponderous with meat. The regulars are irregular and the moss is random. Subjectivity is an illusion. An illusion is subjective. Between the two is a vast realm of predicates, all of them in a predicament of napkins and names. Rocks, animals, everything. Seemingly concrete emotional needs, and Memphis.

We ran down on Westlake today, past all the small businesses by the lake, and passed a dinghy near the entrance to the Discovery Yachts marina that had been repurposed as a planter and was full of white alyssum and purple petunias.

It was a hot afternoon, in the low 70s. Not a searing heat, but enough to make you thirsty and induce a sweat. I couldn't help but notice the high number of morbidly obese people I saw on the walkway and elsewhere. I wonder if that's due to the diminishing nutritional value of our food. In agricultural research, measurements of fruit and vegetables show that their minerals, vitamin and protein content have dropped significantly over the past 50 to 70 years. Industrialized farms have been breeding and choosing bred crops for higher yields rather than nutrition, and high-yielding crops, be it broccoli, tomatoes, or wheat, tend to be less nutrient-rich. People tend to eat more when they're depressed or anxious. Food is comforting. Unless, of course, you're so depressed you don't want to eat at all. I had two hot dogs for dinner. This makes it obvious that nutrition isn't always at the forefront of my appetite. I don't mean to slight the hot dog, which is a mystifyingly satisfying meal, especially if your attention is distracted by something else, in this case episode 113 season 7 of *Seinfeld*, titled "The Maestro," in which Elaine dates a conductor who insists on being called "maestro." I once passed a city conductor when I was out running. He was working on a car and I cracked a joke about him conducting cars which, to gather from his facial expression, was not entirely appreciated. I should've asked if he needed help, although I know less about cars than I do about any musical instrument, including the lowly triangle. As for conducting cars, in the mid-'70s I attended a concert by John Cage at Seattle's Cornish College of the Arts, which ended when Cage took everyone out into the parking lot and conducted a row of cars. People sat inside the cars and were instructed – via Cage's conducting – to turn the volume of the car radio up or down. This constituted the music of the piece, which is titled "Imaginary Landscape no. 4, for 12 Radios." The introduction of cars may have been a new development. I remember the frustrations of listening to AM radio when driving a car in the '60s and '70s; most of the songs were of no interest to me. They were most often saccharine, formulaic, and tame. Then, just when you thought you couldn't take another bubblegum masterpiece, the DJ would play something by the Beatles or Rolling Stones or Bob Dylan and I'd go nuts. The first time I heard "Like a Rolling Stone" was in late August, 1965. I was riding in the back seat of a friend's car. He had a speaker in the back so I was immersed in music. As soon as the first drumbeat and chord were played, I was hooked. It was an exhilarating sound, and the lyrics blew my mind.

There must be more to the mind than brain. The brain is largely soft tissue, gray and white matter, containing nerve cells, non-neuronal cells such as immune cells, glial cells, keratinocytes, stem cells, which synthesize and metabolize steroid hormones and neurotrophic actions under physiological and pathological conditions, such as running and thinking, and regulate synaptic function, affect anxiety, cognition, sleep and behavior, and exert neuroprotective and reparative roles. The brain also consists of small blood vessels and fat. Sixty percent of the content is fat. The rest of it is a matter of some privacy, and sylvan with symbolism and beliefs, some of which are supported by probability, and the others are a jumble of mongrel stone, temples in the jungle, and monkeys in the banyan tree. If the mind were confined to the brain, language would be the only conduit, the only channel by which the mind could contact other minds and create societies of music and mathematics. But what if we consider consciousness as a quality inherent in all matter? Then one's mind would be a vessel interconnecting with other mind energies. You could hear Bach emanating from a blanket, or God thinking in onions. The mind, any given mind, is far too sloppy and steamy to be bounced off the tongue. It can't be caged in a brain like an octopus in the San Francisco aquarium, which, for your information, is open from 11.00 a.m. to 6.00 p.m. most days of the week, but closed on Christmas Eve. Uh-uh: you can't close a mind on Christmas Eve. The mind has needs; it's restless, continuously busy, even in sleep. Inky, an octopus at New Zealand's National Aquarium, slipped out of its tank, slithered down a drainpipe and escaped into the ocean. Isn't that what the mind wants? To slither out of the head and return to the ocean, an oceanic consciousness, a sensation of eternity and bliss, one's self as one with the universe?

The octopus has nine brains, eight in its tentacles, and one enclosed in a cartilaginous skull. The act of thinking is distributed throughout its body. Some cephalopods have spots, like tiny eyes, scattered over the surface of their skin, an organ which appears to be chemically sensitive. What a strange sensation that must be. The cephalopod brain is the most highly developed of any invertebrate. Some have a bead-like light-organ that shines continuously, like a little lamp.

I can never be rid of the image. I see it when I'm not looking at it. It pops up in my mind at unexpected times, triggered by nothing. George Harrison, on the cover of his first album, *All Things Must Pass*, is sitting in a chair on a huge lawn with a stand of evergreens in the background, his estate I assume, and I know he loved gardening and landscaping, and to judge by the big rubber boots that are foregrounded and disproportionately large, he'd been working. The garden gnomes surrounding him are a nice, jocular touch. His big floppy hat seems well matched with the abundance of hair tumbling down and over his shoulders; it seems like part of the garden. I like the image. It feels at home in my head. It always had a weird familiarity for me, having done a lot of yardwork myself. And the misty English cold seems familiar, as that's similar weather to what we have in the Pacific Northwest. I once invested money in an upright piano invention and found out George had made an investment in it too. So I felt a little connected. I never think of him as dead. His music is still going strong. For me, anyway. Occasions to discuss music with people in their 20s are slim. I did have a casual conversation with a twenty-something guy once who'd never heard of Led Zeppelin. I used to wonder, when I was in my 20s, if I'd swing with the times, flow with the zeitgeist, morph into different identities as I progressed with the times. Didn't happen. I still listen to the Beatles. I have no idea what the current hit songs are. But the disinclination among the young to work shit jobs for peanuts, I do understand that.

Anybody can stand in a fountain. But can you do it without getting wet? My point precisely. Hoist anchor and shine. This is a world of integument, not a world of argument. Squeeze the pen when you write, it makes the words come out stronger. Mingle an airport with glitter. Butter an indentation with a meditation. I'm feeling perforated. I tremble to say it, but the drawer is open and you can see all my underwear doing a waltz. I hope it's a waltz. If it's the mashed potato, I don't want to suffer the consequences. There's nothing pretty about a trainwreck of potato peelings. But I love arabesques. This I must admit. You can be in public sometimes and feel like umber is spreading its lumber all over your chatter. Every conversation has its scaffolding. Or the world's most graceful nose. It will keep us talking all night. Everything we know about it will come out of us and shine. Even the mailbox happens by magic. Put your ear close to a brush and hear it bristle. Are the dishes done? Yes, they are. Let's get dressed and get galvanized. Poetry is an engine. But prose is the chassis on which it rolls. I don't care overmuch for representation. It's too complicated. I prefer the immediacy of the unmediated. Ironing, for example. Say a shirt. I can never quite get the collar completely smooth. Or the sleeves or pockets. The back is easy, it spreads nicely on the board. Fun to run the iron over that. So smooth. So giddy. So gherkin. So ghostly. So gesundheit. So giraffe. So completely and utterly giraffe. The intervals between the buttons are impossible. I let that part go. And so it goes. It disappears down the road. And that's the last I will see of my shirt. Or the iron. Or the board. They all went off together wearing the implausible like a shirt, my shirt. I don't blame the fugue, I blame the bravado. Diversions are necessary to live in this world. Everywhere you look there's an entity about to be transmogrified just by looking at it in a certain way. Sometimes oddities are prettier as commodities, which is an abuse of mass. We call this antithesis. The prairies of the Midwest are the antithesis of Wall Street, which is the spinal cord of capitalism. Prairies are places of vast afflatus. The blizzards are pataphysical. So much snow and so much to know. The flakes whirl through the night. Planets glow on the dashboard. The dendrites glow in the mind. Everything small gets bigger and everything big gets smaller. And the world drifts.

Reading an article by William deBuys about the colossal wildfires devouring the forests of the world, I come across the sentence "A bolt of lightning, a fool with a cigarette, a downed power line, or ... goodness knows ... the ham-fisted Forest Service will eventually provide the necessary spark, and then our oxygen planet, warmer and drier than ever, will strut its stuff again." Fifty-six years ago, I was that fool with a cigarette. As a passenger on a drive down I-5 to the Bay Area in my buddy's black '55 Chevrolet sedan, I finished a cigarette and flicked the butt out the window. I remember feeling bad as soon as I did so, the kind of thing done on impulse with nary a thought or quaver of prudence, and hours later forgot about it. The world's hydrologic patterns were reliable and normal back then, and, as far as I know, that cigarette butt didn't cause so much as a small brush fire. But now, 56 years later, I remember the incident with astonishing lucidity, as if I'd just done it. Nor is this an isolated instance. I wince with remorse at a dozen or so remembered acts of negligence, stupidity and reckless folly, per day, sometimes per hour, depending on my mood. Why I focus on all the bad things and none of the good things reveals a proclivity towards the negative, which is a theme for another day. What amazes me in old age, now that I'm in my mid-70s, is the frequency and lucidity of remembering things I never even thought about in my 20s or 30s. It began in my late 60s, this long-term memory thing. It's as if the entire ecology of the brain changed. Why human beings are wired like this, I don't know. Perhaps it's because those of us who have lived this long are in a position to deliver nuggets of wisdom, all of them panned from a brain in which the past flows and chuckles like a mountain stream while the future becomes increasingly veiled and illusory, as vague and chimerical as a sunset obscured by wildfire smoke. And, as is always the case, the young don't listen. I know I didn't. Or I did, and waited later for it to make sense. Fermentation is a long process, optimized at the risk of waste.

I spend a lot of time on the computer, it's true, and I find it dismaying. It's like an ongoing global conversation that allows you to butt in anytime you want. Initially, it went giddy with free speech. This was the heyday of free speech. But then along came politics and riots and persecution and climate catastrophe, and social media went insane. If I have an opinion I'm not shy about sharing it. I'm a fan of opinions. It's like ping pong when you find a person with whom you disagree. It's all about facts. Swatting facts back and forth over a net. In this case, the internet. These are my facts and they're true, you insist. To which your opponent insists their facts are true, I don't know where you got your facts from, out of a cereal box I'll bet. And even this was invigorating and generated thought and inquiry. Lately, though, things have soured dramatically. Now it's all about semantics and tone and shaming and blaming. There are no referees, no umpires, no experts to tell you what to believe or not to believe. Oh, they're there, the experts would have us believe, but if journalists can't decide on who is truly a journalist, then how can the experts agree on their own expertise? The climate of censorship and disinformation and misinformation and propaganda and sources and institutions that can be trusted are virtually nonexistent. I trust a few, but is that my cognitive bias being magnetically drawn into a false objectivity, or a truly unbiased and sound judgment free of any imperious subjectivity? Is there such a thing as objectivity? Does the polarity between subjectivity and objectivity even exist? I believe the quest for knowledge is noble, and to the degree it aspires toward objectivity is truly noble, but objectivity is a chimera. Reality itself is in question. Everything must be viewed through the lens of the Heisenberg Uncertainty Principle. We cannot know both the position and speed of a particle, such as a photon or electron, with perfect accuracy; the more precisely we identify the particle's position, the less we know about its speed. Nor is there any way around the conundrum of altering the phenomenon we're observing by the very act of observing it.

John Locke proposed an interesting experiment. Try holding one hand in ice water and the other hand in hot water for a few moments. Remove both hands simultaneously and put both in a bucket of tepid water. Competing sensations of one and the same objective reality illustrate how two different perceiving minds can have such differing impressions of a single object. Two people could perform this experiment simultaneously and one might describe the tepid water as warm whereas the other person might perceive it as cold. I stumble into discrepancies like this every day. For example, when I'm outside freezing my butt off on a spring day when the temperature is in the upper 50s, and someone remarks about what a beautiful day it is, so spring-like and warm. Or – as happened years ago – that afternoon I met someone who, like me, had just moved to Seattle from California, remarked on how friendly the people in Seattle were. This perplexed me. The only other people I've met more snobbish, stand-offish, cold, impassive, dour, and glum are the people of San Francisco, New York City, and London, England. There were pockets here and there of the eccentrically friendly. But as the computer industry took off and became the juggernaut of Seattle's financial well-being, the tendency toward aloofness morphed into something even stranger, people who were divorced from everything real and wedded to virtual realities, isolating them further from the warm beating heart of the collective, and – like the educated elite of the Isle of Laputa in Jonathan Swift's *Gulliver's Travels* – academic savants so lost in thought they required a servant to walk behind them and hit them softly, generally on the back of the head, with a blown bladder full of pebbles or dry peas, to remind them that they have a body and prevent them from falling into a ditch or walking into a door.

The idea of harvesting data seems like a concept Swift might've come up with. The pairing of those two words, "harvest" and "data" is odd. As if data were a form of barley or soy bean. Dates, maybe. Or the idea of data being a valuable commodity, like silver or gold. What is so valuable about data? It helps companies predict customer behavior. But are people really that predictable? I guess they are. Data miners can modify ads and target them to the exact person who is most likely to make a purchase. But what if that person is Antonin Artaud? He wants an organ for grinding the wind, a triangle of water, a solar donkey, a loud fart, the first euphoria of feeling alive you experienced one day, and a lubricating membrane that floats in the air like a paragraph.

Can Dada be mined? If data can be mined, why not Dada? And what kind of mineral is Dada? Is it a vegetable? Is it cerebral? Is it pertinent or impertinent? Is it crickets or crystals? Is it analogue or dialogue, bitbucket or approximate man, calibration or celebration, coulomb or asylum, diode or tree toad? Binary or nonbinary? Opposition or heat gun? I don't know. But even the most ingenuous communications feel somehow tainted by trade, harvested for its commercial potential. But how could anyone harvest the data of Dada? Dada doesn't have data. Dada is as senseless as applesauce. There are no traits or unique attributes. At best, there is only cart abandonment data. Dada is never serious about anything to which arbitrary values are applied, and all values are arbitrary. Repeated actions, yes, lots of those, but task completion? Come on! Dada is the apotheosis of incompletion. And what are clicks and scrolls? Nonsense. Pure Dada.

The last time I was in a bank was a pleasant experience. Oriana and I joked with the teller who helped us shuffle some money around. We used a coin machine. We brought two big heavy jars full of quarters and nickels and pennies and dimes and fed it to the machine. Full amount came to $160 some dollars. Money is funny. It's always funny. And when it's inflated it gets funnier. Until it's not even money anymore. It's just paper. Or metal. Or a joke. Money has to be respected to be money. The value of the money has to be honored. But when honor and respect take a nosedive and other countries turn their back on the dollar and start trading in foreign currencies, money is hilarious, a sudden inhalation of nitrous oxide, cool to the nose, an Ananda Tandava to the brain. And just to imagine, he said, smiling broadly, I once believed this dollar was worth a dollar. He shakes his head with incredulity. And that was a broker on Wall Street, throwing back shots of scotch.

An amazing array of different shapes and colors on the bathroom counter, which is itself granite and busy with black and gold markings: frisky swirls. Also a soothing, spherical cream-colored jar of vitamin E which I've been using to help heal a burn. Blue and white bottle of Biotène mouth wash. White bar of ivory soap in a brown ceramic soap dish. Nice design, ivory soap. That curve prevents it from sticking to the surface of the soap dish. Blue cap, light yellow jar of Vaseline. Plaid cap of the jar where I put my denture and lozenge of sodium bicarbonate and sodium lauryl sulfate and sundry other chemicals that put the fizz in the effervescence that is Efferdent. Isn't sulfate an area of land ruled by a phosphate? I'm thinking of a caliphate, ruled by a caliph, not a callus. Black can of shaving lather. White ceramic sink, chrome faucets. So much hygiene, so little time.

The bathroom is a fundamental aspect of the mind. It's where we relieve ourselves and make ourselves pretty. It's where we're reminded of our mortality. Serious place, the bathroom. And really what more is there to say about it? I'm a bit shy. Don't get me going. The biggest mystery of the bathroom is the mirror: each time I confront that guy in it and try to give him the sanctuary he needs to brush his teeth and brush his hair and return to the world refreshed, reborn, reiterated, restored, resurrected, and gleaming. Or step out of the shower steaming with warm ablution.

Tonight on the news a fireman referred to the Oak Fire wild-fire southwest of Yosemite Park as "extreme weather behavior." As if fire had a personality and a goal and a need for attention. Those flames do look sinister. Makes you wonder.

Electrical signaling is the basis of our minds. Beans do it. Humans do it. Even beets and broccoli do it. Communicate with electrical signals. The signals are self-propagable and run through each cell to its far end where it stimulates the next cell to generate its own action potential, which runs to the next cell, and so on, carrying the electrical message from cell to cell, making an arm lift, an eye wink, a tongue wag, a nose sniff, ears hear: experiences of touch and temperature to impact the skin and become an image of female beauty. Or an excerpt of God. I've got journeys in my jug, cords in my chords, ripples in my nipples, monarchs in my soup and a strobe-lit lapidary dog named Shlep the Mighty. He's imaginary and runs on a thousand joules of rock.

What is anything written down but a moment captured in words. It dies. It ends there and assumes a different life, the life of the imaginary. The other moment, the original moment, the moment that gave birth and momentum to the moment that got captured by words, is off doing something else, it's already morphed into salmon swimming upstream, each fish struggling against the current. The current that tells them to keep going is the same current that pushes them back. Sounds familiar, doesn't it? Has Albert Camus been here? Did those salmon morph into spikes on a gate in some underworld belonging to a madman or a madcap rockabilly guitarist? The rockabilly underworld can be found along any highway where they have funny hairdos, hot cars, sultry voices and good penmanship. It was something, I tell you. But you had to be there. It was just one of those moments that comes and goes before you were even sure it was there.

I've got a lot of anger. It's been building over the years. I don't think it has as much to do with my personal evolution than the cancerous developments in global societies due to the arrogant and monumentally misguided notions of neoliberal economics and neocon hegemony, which hasn't resulted in anything more than kleptocratic monsters of rapacity and oppression. I try to keep my anger to myself as much as I can, which isn't particularly healthy, but it prevents me from destroying what's left of my social existence. Most people find anger off-putting. This is normal. Not a big surprise. I have no argument against it. Anger is frowned on in most industrialized nations. Its disruptions erode profit. Its honesty is destabilizing. It runs contrary to the positivity movements that keep people in denial and the capitalist machine running smoothly. That said, I see anger as a positive, not a negative, emotion. It's gasoline. It's diesel. It's a driver of change. It's also what made Bill Hicks such a great comedian. Anger is a goldmine of humor.

Anger isn't easy to corral. I don't like feeling it all the time. That's exhausting. Anger is hard to manage. Anger isn't a neutral and malleable energy that can be directed in various ways. It's not an affect that one can easily monopolize. It's a rodeo, and you're a cowboy trying to ride it and keep from being hurled to the ground. Appeasement is futile. Look for pressure valves.

On hot days like this (84 degrees at 6.52 p.m.) I take my hat off to the refrigerator. It never goes on vacation, never calls in sick. It spends 24 hours 7 days a week humming and clicking and humming and rattling along, keeping everything inside cool and fresh. I don't have a hat, but is there reason to mention that detail? I think there is. Details are important. They're the peppermint of the big picture, which on any given day is too abstract for tongs. It can only be handled by experts with the right gloves. And the fabric and make of these gloves is a vital detail, and kept in a vault, the combination and proportions of which are known only to the Dalai Lama.

Intersection, transfer, emergence, and paradox are central to life. Remarked British geologist Nigel Thrift, who, in 2018, was appointed Chair of the Committee on Radioactive Waste Management. I agree. I believe this observation is pertinent to writing also, which is an ecology of words, nostrums and rosaries of words, forests of words, intersecting, transferring, emerging, and paradoxical words. Very unlike, in fact, Mussolini's Fascist forest on the slope of Mount Giano, near the little town of Antrodoco. The forest is made up of 20,000 black Austrian pine saplings, planted to spell out DVX, Mussolini's title in Latin. The imposition of trees not native to the area makes it extremely vulnerable to disease and fire, and most likely it won't survive. Paradox is crucial to the vibrancy and resilience of systems. Without paradox, it is impossible to say what a true miracle a tree is, or a spice, or a spider, or a sibilant hissing out of a delicious incongruity. For example, this statement is a lie. It is also insanely logical.

There is no such thing as an organism that is separate from other organisms. This should not require explanation. But look at yourself. Look at your fingers. Look at your legs. Look at your eyes. Look at your nose. Look at the veins in your hand. Look at the lake. Look at the shore beneath your feet. Look at the light. Look at the dark. Look at the light within the dark. Look at the darkness within the light. Look at the waves in your breath. Feel the muscles of the neck when you swallow a sip of juice or a morsel of food. Look at the food. Where did the food come from? Watch the swallows. Study the hollows. Which of these things could exist without water, atoms and molecules, DNA, a planet, an ocean, minerals, sediments, impediments, and interwoven melodies? I didn't invent or create a single piece of myself, including my sense of self, which is the most illusory thing about me, however real it feels, which is a product of reading, and talking, and all the various ruses I use to query the exquisite pain of being alive.

I always have the feeling that I don't know what I'm doing, especially when I'm trying to repair something, a flush valve, or a hole in a wall. I always feel so inept when I go about these things. I like doing things for which I feel a small degree of competence, and won't get my fingers sticky, or become a source of embarrassment. I could try to write a Shakespearean sonnet; that would make me feel better. I gave up on the guitar a long time ago but I don't fret about it. I fixed the blues with a judicious use of green. I try to stay tidy, that way I minimize the chance of tripping on something and breaking a bone. Here's my philosophy in a nutshell: if it ain't broke, don't fix it. Not Plato, no, but it'll do in a pinch. I found it in a used bookstore and fixed it with some duct tape. Here are some things that can be fixed with duct tape: tents, hoses, recalcitrant warts, lunar module filtration systems or a toilet seat. Hope I've been of use. I feel better already.

It's been an unusually hot day today. The high was 87. In the evening, after dinner, I watch the French news on my laptop, *Le journal de France 2 vingt heures*. I listen to it in French for two reasons, the first being my ongoing struggle to learn French and the joy of hearing it spoken, the second being the obliqueness of getting a view of the world through another country. I have nothing but disgust for what passes as journalism in the United States. It's all lies and propaganda, information biased in favor of powerful corporate entities, the technocracy in particular, and the military-industrial complex. The news in France also, I'm sure, reflects a corporate bias, but it's significantly less aggressive, a little less distorted, and centered more around human communities. The news tonight is particularly terrifying and has to do with the severe megadrought France has been experiencing. The segment, entitled *Climat: la sécheresse sévit toujours dans 93 départements* (Climate: drought still rages in 93 departments), shows two satellite images of France. The one from just a year ago shows a country that is still largely green. The other shows it yellowed by the lack of water. They haven't had such low levels of precipitation since 1959. Currently, precipitation is at a few millimeters to almost zero. Rivers, including the Loire, have dried up. Their beds are caked mud with threads of water trickling through. The crops in fields are dry, short, and brittle, barely any life to them at all. The dirt is more dust than dirt.

The situation in the U.S. isn't much better. California and the southwest have been devasted by drought and wildfires. Lake Mead and Lake Powell could feasibly be gone in a few months. The future of food in our grocery stores is beginning to look increasingly threatened.

It's hard getting mustard in France. The problem is seeds. A shortage of seeds affects the whole planet. Canada, the world's largest supplier, experienced a historic drought last summer that destroyed a third of its mustard seed production.

Because I love mustard, this is a worry. Among many other worries. Worry has become the mustard seasoning my life. The yellow spicy flavor of worry that roils the static of my hot dog.

Mustard is all over the New Testament. In Matthew, for example, 13:31-32, "He presented another parable to them, saying, 'The kingdom of heaven is like a mustard seed, which a man took and sowed in his field; and this is smaller than all other seeds, but when it is full grown, it is larger than the garden plants and becomes a tree, so that the birds of the air come and nest in its branches.'"

This is true: the mustard seed becomes a tree. I didn't know that.

It fascinates me no end that colossal sequoias and redwood

come from tiny seeds – and by tiny I mean minuscule, about the size of a pinhead. There are many implications to be drawn from that. What was the seed out of which Victor Hugo's *Les Miserables* grew? Or the House of Grimaldi? How many palimpsestic layers in a single word?

"Longing is like the seed / That wrestles in the ground / Believing if it intercede / It shall at length be found." Emily Dickinson.

If words could repair the world, I would if I could make everything wood.

And sometimes I wonder how such beautiful sounds may be extracted from a set of strings and an arrangement of wood. It isn't rhythm or timpani or texture or tremolo, it isn't harmony or melody or mode or volume, though they're part of it. It's the notes. Single notes. Brought together so fluently they seem like one and the same membrane, a tenuity of webs and cymbals developing diminuendos, furbishing gongs, modulating octaves, rounding rubato, swinging tempo, then crashing it all together with flutes and falsettos. But really, that isn't it either. Not the essence of the thing, the noumenon, the phenomenal side of things, things that are ineffable and cannot be described. Description kills the ineffable. It's like pinning a butterfly to a mounting board. Beautiful to look at, but dead. The reality of reality is in its unreality. You can't throw a net of words over it, because if you do it will reinvent your net, turn into music and escape.

An apricot is not a snowball. The storm is a breath fleeing the lungs of an angry universe. Saturday's parable is Sunday's dragon of pearls. The heart is crammed with a piercing emotion, and so becomes thunder in a mountain sink. The forest looks funny on a woman's knee, so helpless and uncontrolled. The algebra cat has solved itself with a mean deviation. There's a grayish piece of roof around my decade. Whatever happened to scarabs? There's an unknown color somewhere in the retina of a plow. The weight of loving is counterbalanced by the symmetry of obsession. The wind's membrane is metal. But when it lifts it becomes the fast taste of anything streaming across your shoulder. And this has calories, four hundred fingers wiring a chocolate Monday to a little gnarled faucet. I strip down to get dressed in my memory of time and discover Luxembourg in my mirror, smiling like a plumber with a gold tooth and a wrench.

Who was it said writers are God's spies? God being the corporation of the sky. Which manufactures clouds and dreams. And floats in people's hearts like a slingshot. Full of stipends. These may be stipulated or stippled, like stilettos, or storms. But spies, yes. It was King Lear, talking to Cordelia: "No, no, no! Come, let's away to prison. / We two alone will sing like birds i'th' cage. / When thou dost ask me blessing, I'll kneel down / And ask of thee forgiveness. So we'll live, / And pray, and sing, and tell old tales, and laugh / At the gilded butterflies, and hear poor rogues / Talk of court news; and we'll talk with them too – Who loses and who wins; who's in, who's out – / And take upon 's the mystery of things, / As if we were God's spies; and we'll wear out, / In a wall'd prison, packs and sects of great ones / That ebb and flow by th' moon."

Spies are skilled at observing things without drawing attention. They do it by blending in. They do it without letting on that they're observing. Catching details. The quality and size of a sheet of paper, its thickness and texture, its fiber, its submission to the flow of a pen.

The tonsil, too, is a tool. And the tongue is utter poker. Menus are the chronicles of the food and predilection of our time. But the jukebox is rare, and hides in a corner where the hits sleep in vinyl until they're awakened by a needle sliding through their grooves. Well, it's been building up inside of me for, oh, I don't know how long. I don't know why, either, but I keep thinking that something is bound to go wrong. Because it always does. Shit happens. So why worry about it? Worry, I've heard said, is like trying to solve a math problem by chewing gum. And the hits keep coming. I stuffed that monster with quarters. Teenage angst. Adult angst. And the angst of old babies that nurse their worries in gin and rock their equations on stools and stare longingly at the mirror.

Gunslinger in a golden vest playing an electric guitar like it was a clitoral entry to paradise.

"Let's all try to learn a few things and pick each other up when we're down and not ever push nobody down because we're up."
Stevie Ray Vaughan, October 3, 1954 – August 27, 1990.

What was I doing on August 27, 1990? It was a Monday, so I was probably feeling a bit glum about returning to work. Though admittedly, and to a small but discernible degree, I enjoyed that short wait at the bus stop by Jimmy Woo's Jade Pagoda on Capitol Hill, leaning against a brick retaining wall, amenable to the moment, mulling whatever happened to be fomenting in my mind. It was a pretty neighborhood before the developers got there and destroyed its charm with unaffordable apartment buildings with hard right-angles and bland façades devoid of aesthetic play. That was an odd interlude in my life. It also involved going to a coffeehouse called The Last Exit, which was on Brooklyn, and had tables of marble slabs that had once been stall dividers in the old King County Courthouse. There were always chess games going, hands bonking timers, and conversations by which you could obtain an education if you listened in casually. I'd read a little Kerouac, or Proust, or Celine, then trudge to work. The whole sequence functioned as an airlock, giving me time to ready my resolve, noodle my poodle, open the door, and do time.

It takes time to kill time. So don't kill all of it. Leave some for the time being.

Louis C.K. has a joke about time travel into the future. The joke is simple: it's what happens when you age. It's how I feel a lot of the time: like a traveler from the mid-20th century visiting Planet Earth in the second decade of the new millennium. I didn't require a machine, I just aged, stayed alive long enough to get here. I wish I could go back. Return to, say, 1968 and warn everyone of the horrors then in the making that could be avoided. I can see it as a movie. I run around frantically trying to warn people. Listen! Hear me speak! I will shout. Gather round, for I am from the future, and here's what I saw: sidewalk zombies hunched, heads bent down, controlled by the tiny machines in their hands. ebikes and escooters and monowheels driven at breakneck speed by goggled mutants swathed in leather. Clerks at the stores who no longer say hello or smile. They don't like being there and they're not above letting you know that. It's not a friendly place. A lot of people have dogs. The dogs substitute for the lack of community. There will be billionaires in possession of such astronomical wealth they'll host parties in space and control world governments. This will contrast with a huge population of homeless people living in tents. Twelve gallons of gas will be 50 bucks. "You will own nothing and be happy," said Klaus Schwab.

I'm looking at a world with gazillions of little twinkly dots all around it, save for a bald spot near the north pole. It looks like a mess, like a disease of astrophysical proportions. It's a projection of what the space around Planet Earth will look like after Elon Musk has finished sending satellites into space. The project, called Starlink, began in 2019 when Musk began launching satellites by Falcon rockets in clusters of 50, some of which are visible from earth at night. They look like lines dotted with lights. The object is to offer high speed internet connectivity, even in the most isolated regions. Once positioned in orbit, the satellites will deploy solar panels for energy. The full number will be somewhere in the neighborhood of 42,000. Some people worry that they'll heighten the risk of collisions.

D'ya think?

It reminds me a little of all the houses and shrubbery festooned with lights at Christmas. Christmas ceased being a favorite holiday sometime after my 13th birthday. It became increasingly stressful until, sadly, in old age with nearly all our family members gone, it's now relatively peaceful. It feels shameful to admit that, but it's true. The pressure is off. I can sit on the couch with Oriana and stare into space, like Molly does. No need for presents or small talk. Nothing but the stillness of the long December night.

I've never understood New Year's Eve celebrations. I understand celebrations. I like celebrations. I'm willing to celebrate anything. Static Electricity Day. Marzipan Day. Thesaurus Day. Backwards Day. Ferris Wheel Day. Alfred Hitchcock Day. Haiku Day. Zipper Day. I could spend a lifetime celebrating things day by day. Cats, erasers, egg yolks. Buttons, wigs, underwear. But time? It's so abstract, so arbitrary. Why not celebrate 2.00 p.m.? Six p.m.? Midnight?

Time can tear down a building or destroy a woman's face.

Hours are like diamonds, don't let them waste. Sings Mick Jagger.

I would like to acknowledge this moment with a sparkly paper hat, a firecracker, and a fifth of gin.

I always liked Thanksgiving. That's a good one. All you have to do is eat. Be polite. Avoid political discussions. Or religion. All you have to do is be thankful. I can be thankful. And if I'm not feeling it, not feeling genuinely thankful, I can pretend to be thankful, I can get some white meat on my fork and look around a table and smile. You can't argue with meat. Meat is meat. Happily met. Diligently chewed.

Sometimes an artificial emotion is better than no emotion at all. Wear a plume and become a multitude. Gratitude goes where the current is swift and the bottom glares back in specks of gold.

Why turkey? Why eat so much food? Why watch football? Why try to make conversation with a full mouth and a vigorous inner policing of one's thoughts? There's an artistry to it. Like walking a tightrope with a paintbrush in one hand and a fund of facts in the other. Which you would be a fool to use. Use your instincts. Use a fork. Use a spoon. Clean your plate. Help clear the table. And when you arrive home free of obligations and sigh, close the door and dream of Innisfree, and a small cabin build there, of clay and wattles made, and Beatles CDs, and a globe of brandy with your fingers curled under it, warming it, as would Yeats, I imagine, in us free.

When in Australia, out in the bush, be sure to clap your hands to scare off the spring snakes.

That's the best advice I can give the youth of today. That,

and these lines from Rosie and the Originals: It's just like heaven being here with you.

I will arise now and go to the kitchen, to feed the cat, and visit the bathroom on the way back. There's a towel there I'd like you to meet, I say to my hands, which are eager hands, eager to grasp, eager to touch, eager to fold and be folded, like the shadows at noon, which are folded into shrubbery and disappear behind the barn, only to reappear a few minutes later holding a genera of stem succulents, like the euphorbias of the desert, fixing CO_2 almost exclusively at night, and trading it in on a horse and carriage. I commend them for their bravery, for their nimbleness, and for their dexterity, which is a pretext for squeezing your pretzel and stealing your watch. Legerdemain, man. It stole my city. And won my hand in marriage.

Ollie Polly, a polymorphic polynomial from Polysyndeton, Idaho, comes to visit me and leaves me with a tiny pellet of paper saying "Happy Birthday," then, responding at once to the call of a polyzoan, rises up in a great flourish of wings and bells and flies out the window and disappears into a black speck over the summit of Mount Rainier. I put the pellet in a teacup of water, as Ollie advised, stood back, and watched as it expanded and unfolded into an exact replica of the Crystal Palace for the 1851 Great Exhibition. I looked around the apartment for somewhere to put it, somewhere we won't step on it in the middle of the night, and realized we were living in it, our entire apartment was now on exhibit, and I turned to smile and wave at the people walking by, the men dressed in frock coats and the women in dome-shaped skirts, twirling parasols and giggling. I blew Queen Victoria a kiss and pressed the world against my heart.

Those weird moments in the morning when the problem

presented to you in a dream keeps troubling you until you realize it was a dream and the problem has no reality. Now, apply that to actual problems, rub them hard with the balm of nonsense and watch them sigh on the verge of verisimilitude, exhilarated with their newfound unreality, and ready to jump into the wilderness, and engage in its many activities, and get by on vagrancy and yoga, until somebody solves them by illustrating the superfluity of the problem, which isn't really a solution but a way to stare at the sea.

A skeleton sat in front of a radio in Lassitude, Wyoming, listening. Listening to listening. Listening to the music of the spheres. Physicists say the sun sounds like the roar of Niagara Falls. The wise urge us to hear the music inside ourselves. No note should be a knot. Keep it loose. Keep it pure. Keep it purring. And keep it going. Soliloquys are frightening on Halloween. An eerie sound of anguish can clear the street in a Gothic minute. We can light the silence with bells. And this will help you get better acquainted with the entertainment industry, which begins in your mind; that's where the real circus is. The women in glittery tights on percherons. The men on the flying trapeze. Gregory Corso in a red coat with epaulets and tassels of gold waving a malacca cane at the top of the big top, where the muses open their wings and ascend into the night to do their dirty business, keeping people hunched over a kitchen table, writing furiously.

Dressed and ready to go for a run, I step out into the hallway and go up the steps and stand and gaze at the play of light on the shale tile of the landing by the entrance to our building. It looks like the shimmer of diaphanous folds of solar gauze and evokes the presence of something preternatural, angelic or ghostly. Oriana appears and puts on her running shoes. Another hot day. A few feet away from our building, she informs me that she just saw one of our next-door neighbors naked on the balcony patio. She wasn't sure if it was a man or a woman. I suspect it was a man as I'd just heard a man's voice talking on a mobile phone. He was behind the poplars and I couldn't see him. This person must not realize they're in full view of a crowded neighborhood. Or just not care. Maybe he's from Sweden.

Another hot day. This is why we left earlier than usual, 10.00 a.m. It was already 75 degrees Fahrenheit. I saw the same guy as yesterday covered head to toe in tattoos, shirt off, pushing a baby buggy. He smiled. Friendly guy. Funny if the baby had tattoos.

We return home and I pour some coffee from the thermos. Wonderful invention, the thermos.

We hear a jet fly overhead. It sounds like one of the Blue Angels. They appear every year at this time for Seattle's Seafair Parade – which also involves a big hydroplane race on Lake Washington – and perform aerial maneuvers over the city. None of these interest us much, neither the Blue Angels roaring overhead in a tight Delta Formation or a Delta Breakout or a Back-to-Back Pass. Or the roar of motorboats designed to derive lift from the water and behave more like airplanes than boats, with an enormous Lycoming T-55 L-7 turbine engine looming forward just behind the cockpit. Or the parade itself, with its dazzling array of floats and the hijinks of the Seafair Pirates kidnapping toddlers and trafficking wives. The hydroplanes can be ignored. The Blue Angels cannot. They fly overhead at a very low altitude, low enough to see the pilot in his cockpit. On more than one occasion I thought one of them was going to fly right up my ass. They were canceled – as was the hydroplane race – for those two years when Covid was most active. Odd. A virus so small it's invisible to the naked eye silenced our skies for two years.

Are all civilizations this much in love with war? War seemed pretty exciting to me as a kid. It's all I thought about. I used to draw pictures of fighter planes then shoot them down with my pencil shooting bullets of graphite. I lost my romance with war at about age 14. Not sure what brought that about. Maybe it was my discovery of masturbation – a colossal discovery! – or becoming jaded with fighter planes after gluing so many models together.

I had one interest at age 15: alcohol. It was far and away the most amazing discovery of my life up to that point. Occasions for enjoying this product were sorely limited by my inability to purchase it. Thus I entered a phase of existence in which I'd spend hours sitting in parking lots by minimarkets and taverns with my buddies hoping some guy over 21 would purchase a bottle of whiskey or a case of beer for us. It was on such occasions that I discovered the joy and utility of conversation.

The third great discovery of my adolescence was Shakespeare. I took to him immediately. It was like discovering a psychedelic plant, a linguistic ayahuasca, a peyote in iambic pentameter. It gave my mind greater wingspan. I could hover over the frontier of life – such as I knew it at age 16 – with ease and alacrity, noting all of its tragedy and humor and how weirdly intertwined they were. It wasn't just an intellectual pleasure, it was physical. It made me feel more nimble, quicker on my feet, and more alert. The focus on negotiating the hazards and complexities of life with adroit maneuvers of linguistic expression helped reinforce an immunity to chaos. Immunities work by vaccinating the body with the particles of the disease. Shakespeare works by ingestion as well, diffusing into the blood the DNA of the English language and all of its manias and nostrums.

I like to get naked and get into the refrigerator and imagine

I'm food. The possibilities are endless, like cheese. Take, for example, the ice cube. I think of it as a glass structure for growing sacred songs. The door opens, the light goes on, and the pure beauty of the cube is unleashed on the world, even as it melts in a glass of ice tea while reading "The Drunken Boat" by Arthur Rimbaud. An amazing poem, unaffected as suds in a kitchen sink, and yet iridescent, like the whirls on a single bubble, floating you out of your mind. Next destination: Nicaragua, and the silky seeds of the ceiba. The tree is great that knows itself with utter confidence. I see mutations pulse in the syllables of time like rain as a woman in a black shawl walks down a street in Granada. Can you name all the dimensions of the afternoon? I see one now, transparent as a dream hanging from a window frame, dripping slow rhythms under the drone of daylight.

Old people are often cautioned not to spend too much time in the sun. And if they must be in the sun, to be careful to cover themselves or smear their skin with sunscreen. There is something remotely vampiric about this. Vampires hate daylight. Why is that? Is it because our time on earth is coming to a close and the grave somberly awaits our return to the underworld?

Funny, the things that go on with the skin when people get old. Wrinkles, obviously. But also skin lesions, psoriasis, pigmentary changes, blistering disorders, warts and moles.

Our histories are written on the skin. Look at Keith Richards. The man has a huge library. And he himself is a library.

Keith Richards cracks me up. Every time I see his face now, I laugh. I've never encountered anyone so blithely indifferent to their appearance, to how much age has transformed the dark brooding face of a young man with a legendary history of drug abuse, chiefly heroin and alcohol, into the craggy, heavily wrinkled face of a man now in his late 70s, still performing, and – what's more, now that he's quit smoking, performing with force and unabashed glee – fills me with humor and admiration.

Skin: it's all there. Largest organ of the body. It becomes a parchment in old age. It gets weird. Behaves strangely. I noticed a minuscule protrusion on my jaw while shaving. It's barely noticeable, but I worry about these things. I thought it might be a wart. It's not. The doctor said it was a mole. A mole is caused by a cluster of melanocytes, usually as a result of prolonged exposure to sunlight. I'm outdoors a lot because of my running. Sunlight's the culprit. And age.

What's the difference between a wart and a mole? A mole likes coffee and a wart plays mahjong with your skin. There should be songs about warts. There should be operas about moles. Moles are intrinsically ornamental, and can sometimes enhance a woman's beauty. Warts are repugnant and seem tethered to the supernatural. Warts are the lunatic flowerings of the human papilloma virus. They adorn the faces of witches and wizards like a node of affliction. I wonder what it's like being a dermatologist. So many diseases: acne, hives, diaper rash, eczema, shingles, rosacea, cellulitis, impetigo, erysipelas. But all up front, right there were you can see it. Skin is a window to infection in other bodily systems. The pinprick lesions which do not blanche when a clear glass is pressed on them can alert doctors to meningitis or meningococcal septicemia.

Skin is a connective tissue. At night when I search for a bottle of water I guess its position on the table and then feel for its distinctive shape and texture, the rills that lend assistance to my fingers.

It does connect me. But not like a plug. Not like a port in a laptop. It's not wired to anything. The connection is more of a fusion than a contact, a benediction of the permeable, a chorus for the porous. Skin is sensitive to temperature. Fluids enter and emerge by osmosis. What if the universe were one big cube of jello? The universe is a sphere of dark energy, dark matter, nonstop chatter and bones and pomegranates with a radius of 14 billion light years and a radio that is always tuned to Wolfman Jack. It's a busy place, but never too busy for skin, skin is its own best advertisement for leisure, which is holy, and feels fantastic in a reclining armchair.

I never get over the astonishingly acute sense of warmth and aliveness when I touch another human being, be it a handshake, a kiss, or the warmth of Oriana's hand.

Tattoos are one of the oldest forms of art. A book on clinical dermatology would make a really bad coffee table book. But a book on tattoos would be quite an intimate experience, especially if it were written on somebody's body. But what if you wanted to read it on a bus? Or check it out from the library? I still haven't read *Adventures in the Skin Trade*. I'll bet it's touching.

It's 11.10 a.m. and we just returned from a little walk outside with Molly. She's an indoor cat, so to be outside is the equivalent of an astronaut landing on a distant planet. Everything she sees from the vantage point of our living room window, which is level with the ground, sparrows and robins and squirrels and – horror of horrors – other neighborhood cats, she is now experiencing up close and personal. The neurons in her brain must be rapid-firing with a thousand curiosities and speculations about the world. Oriana has on a pair of gardening gloves. The last time she took our cat outside and our cat freaked out and she tried picking her up she got mauled. I accompanied them this time and Molly was much calmer. She was doing fine, sniffing at plants and ambling along in the rather tightfitting harness she wears outdoors, until the mailman arrived. He's a friendly guy but a complete stranger to our cat. She went immediately for the door to our building. That's a good sign. If she ever gets out on her own, she'll know where to go. On balance, it was a successful mission. Hopefully, it will help to quell her boredom and distract her from begging for food all day.

Another river in France has dried up. This time it's the Drôme, a tributary of the Rhône, in southeastern France. Everyone agrees that this is the first time they've seen anything like it, and that – as a product of climate change and the worsening of drought conditions – it's unlikely to improve. We all live on a different planet now, different from the one on which we were born.

Elsewhere, in Texas, the heat and lack of rain have uncovered dinosaur tracks from 113 million years ago. The tracks are deep and clearly visible in what used to be the Paluxy River, a tributary of the legendary Brazos. It was a bipedal animal of considerable weight, identified as a therapod called Acrocanthosaurus, which stood about 15 feet tall and weighed close to seven tons. There's an irony in this discovery. The dinosaurs went extinct due to abrupt climate change, a brief but dramatic rise in temperature caused by the impact of an asteroid. We're now dealing with another possibly fatal impact, though the asteroid in this case is us – 8.0 billion of us. The optimal number of people for a planet this size is in the vicinity of 1.5 to 2 billion. Humanity is gobbling up resources – soil and water to grow food, coal and wood and natural gas to provide heat, iron or copper to make cooking pans, lithium for phones and cars, cobalt for jet planes, platinum for telecommunications and jewelry, chromium for stainless steel and leather treatment, zinc oxide for sunscreen – at a rate 1.8 times faster than our planet's biocapacity can regenerate.

The planet I grew up on is gone. The new planet is unfolding a new set of problems, not just for humankind, but everything, the whole ball of wax, plants and trees and lizards and fish. Eons of evolution are about to be rendered obsolete. It's a strange new feeling, both mournful and electrifying. It calls for desperate measures. But apart from the preppers and their collection of food staples and traps and guns, what can anybody do? I try to be ... I don't know what to call it. I won't call it fatalistic, that's too glib. The entire situation is unprecedented. It's like being in a blizzard in the middle of nowhere, an expanse of long flat highway in the Midwest, and your car breaks down and the heater goes off and there's no plan of action other than to sit and wait for something to gel before you freeze to death, and you fill with frustration and anger because you have to admit – you can't suppress the feeling – the scene is as sublime as it is beautiful.

Pain is rarely concise. It screams for elaboration. But that's not saying anything of help to anyone. Pain needs to distance itself from easy answers if it is to be strummed and turned into a song. It needs the oxygen of the open highway to resolve its ambiguities. But until then it's just you and the cracked old voice of Bob Dylan. The desert smells of sage. The desert is a woman whose voluptuousness is protected by an array of needles. A cactus, yes, but also a terrycloth towel and all the comfort that can bring in a cheap motel. Every perfume has its source in ancient mysteries. Life can be enjoyed as a sideshow with a bearded lady and a man who is half alligator, but if you want the full show you've got to accept some pain along the way. Meanwhile, it is my privilege to inform you that the curtains are drawn and there's some laudanum on the dresser.

And to think we were almost angelic, or so it seemed during the Renaissance, and the portrayals of painters such as Fra Angelico, whose angels are golden-haired beings with flawless complexions and beautifully ornate wings, an exaltation of all that is sublime in the human spirit, quite unlike the creatures we now see in baggy shorts and flip flops.

Almost: it's got disappointment written all over it. Sad, sad word. You were close. You were almost there. Almost succeeded. Almost got the job. Almost won the contest. Almost scored a point. Almost made the basket. Almost kissed her. Almost had the right answer. Almost made it to the other side. Almost got off the ground. Almost learned the drums. Sad word, yes, though there's a slightly more benign meaning to it as well, a mitigating imbalance. Almost tripped. Almost lost my job. Almost shit my pants. Almost fell off. Almost got hit. Almost missed my line. Almost got the job which, though greatly disappointing at the time, opened the way to getting a part in a play called *Almost Always Allspice*, which led to a movie and an Oscar, which I almost won.

It's all about patterns. Isn't it? I'm amazed by all these mirrors and doors. They all seem so well-organized you'd swear you were in a paradisiacal hotel in the middle of a gargle. How does one go about furnishing such rooms? I use hummingbirds and string. It was the images that drew me into writing parallels. I loved it as a kid when I saw how photographs developed, and today that fascination has led to a collection of stuff I've forgotten the name of. I can't remember a time without reflections. Let me tell you a little story. Once, I was obsessed with wealth. I used money sauce for the meat of the moment, which was sizzled in a pan of gold. And then I threw it all away. Why, you ask. Because money talks. It whispers success when you're living a lie. Then it curls around a spine and walks on its hands to the door. That's when you know, and know for sure, the big road is heavy with foundries, but if you feel the need to be where the sky reaches into space, where everything feels open and there's nothing symmetrical or cynical or too direct, and everything is clouds, and diffuse and kind, you should go. You should rise on the merit of your inclinations. Just be sure to bring a change of clothes and hang something bright and metallic around your neck. Remember: patterns. It's all about patterns. And plumbing and soap.

We all understand iron. We know what it does, what it can do to a person. It can make them willful and self-absorbed, like Robert Downey, Jr as industrialist Tony Stark, or chronically ironic, like a postmodern art critic. Don't just stand around: go. Rub your nerves with rubies of sound. Get in a car and don't look back. Not till you get to Michigan. My memory is a heavy net. I remember the thunder of North Dakota, and what my stomach felt like after riding in a small plane. It felt rough. And exciting. Mostly exciting. With more than a bit of life in the sensation. And now it's here. We can sense it. Feel it in our gut. There's a hot molecular morning at the window. We need to reassemble it. Create some energy and restore it to its original position before it blew up right in front of us. When we were slashing one another's tires. And too tired to look inside and see what was happening to ourselves. So, yeah, bring whatever you want to the table. Stomp around in trinkets and bells. The bean is pleading for hydrants and the drums are pounding rhythms of glee and seesaw. The mouth is glue on Saturday. There's so much to say I can't say it, I have to put it in a letter. Consider this the letter. Dear Whoever, let's meet up and talk. We could both use a break. It's cold out tonight and there's a bonfire at the end of the street.

Uh oh. Here they come. Fucking Blue Angels. Time to get my noise-canceling earphones on.

Why is everything by Bach so energetic? He must've drunk a lot of coffee. Every composition is an intermingling pattern of counterpoint and melodies playing off one another, busily, like wood grains, like oak. Oak: wonderful wood. Hard, dense, enduring. An oak in Dresden that survived the WWII fire bombing by U.S. forces is over 300 years old. It's called *Splittereiche* (Splintered Oak) because of a gash in it caused by shrapnel. Bach visited Dresden a number of times. On December 1st, 1736, shortly after his appointment as *Kapellmeister von Haus aus* (Kapellmeister from home) to the Dresden court, he gave a recital on the recently completed Silbermann organ in the Frauenkirche. The *Splittereiche* would've been 14 years old, a teenager. Strange time of life for a human. Maybe not so much for an oak. Do oaks sneer? They do not. Do oaks brood? Maybe. I suspect this particular oak may have done a lot of brooding after 1945.

I vaguely understand it. I've always been drawn to basements. They fascinate me. They're always so different from the rest of a house, either neglected completely and full of mold and spider webs, or happy places, where you can cut loose, play music and dance. I imagine a basement in which a chandelier hangs from a ceiling of big wooden beams and a cubbyhole for cuckoos. And this would be like Bach's "The Gallina" (or Cuckoo), for three bassoons. It would be played in a basement on a day full of mist and nuance, when the day is full of cracks and irregularities and portals to other dimensions. You can feel the joyful suck of sexual caverns and there are no real boundaries between inner life and outer life. Existence becomes phenomenal and charged when we're standing on the shore of an island in the Aegean Sea holding a shield and the moment is galvanized with the tacit understanding of gods and invisible powers. These are the adventures of the basement, where the unconscious is king and nothing is forbidden.

But this is beside the point, which I lost so long ago I can't remember if there was a time when I had a point, or felt a point, or pursued a point, or felt like developing a point, until it became pointless, and I came to a rest and felt the arbitrariness of life pulse in rhythms that accelerated my perception of time, which is the most arbitrary thing in the universe, a hyperobject whose minions are clocks and whose dimensions are varied, like the toes of the human foot.

Today is August 4th. The Blue Angels are out to rehearse their moves for Seattle Seafair. Must be a bit challenging today; visibility is less than optimal. The weather is chilly and gray, more like March than August. Oriana went out earlier for her morning walk. When she returned, she reported seeing Louise, the crow with the bad leg. She's been getting a bit fussy about where she wants to be fed. Louise ignored the first few peanuts tossed on the corner of Bigelow and Highland, where a woman who dyes her hair purple lives, and flew instead to 3rd Avenue, which is a little more secluded, and there she came down to eat her peanuts. Next time we're out we should toss some peanuts to the Blue Angels. Everybody likes peanuts except kids with peanut allergies. They probably like peanuts, but can't eat them. Not without consequences.

I don't understand allergies. I understand they're a hypersensitive response of the immune system to typically harmless substances, but how does that happen? Weirdly, it has something to do with being overprotected, living in too sheltered an environment, so that the immune system isn't exposed to enough pathogens to keep itself busy and so begins attacking harmless antigens and normally benign microbial objects. Strange paradox: too much protection proves harmful. This seems to be an area where poor kids get an advantage and rich kids get peanut allergies.

Mr Peanut nods his head sagely. Rigged out in top hat, cane and monocle, he looks aristocratic. Not a snobby aristocrat but a benign and cheerful aristocrat with an all-embracing philosophy. Good to know that as a member of the *Arachis hypogaea* family he remains somewhat neutral on class distinctions. What is humbler than peanut butter? But did you know that in a high-pressure environment peanut butter can be turned into diamonds? Understanding comes in fragments.

Mosaics. I don't think I've said enough about mosaics. The world's largest mosaic is 9,000 square feet and was discovered in Antakya, Turkey while digging the foundation for a new hotel. It depicts intricate geometric and figural designs crafted from thousands of small stone tesserae. The mosaic was incorporated into the hotel, allowing (I love this phrase) "a peek at history." As if history were a dainty woman getting dressed behind a partition embellished with song birds. History isn't dainty. History is a mosaic of monads and shifting paradigms. History is a kaleidoscopic chaos of blood and conquest, dinosaurs and dynamite, women and children cowering in fear as bombs drop, or mounted horsemen come riding through town flailing swords. History is rust and ruins and walls erected and walls torn down. John Keats, his coughing lulled by a bit of laudanum, sitting under a tree writing an ode to a nightingale. Shakespeare writing "the rest is silence" as his main character, Hamlet, dies in Horatio's arms. Galileo, peering through a refracting telescope consisting of a convex objective lens and a concave eyepiece, discovers moons orbiting Jupiter. April 27th, 1937: the last rivet is inserted into the Golden Gate Bridge. 20:05 GMT, 20 July 1969, the lunar landing module sets down on the moon. November 24th, 1974, Tom Gray and Donald Johanson driving a Land Rover outside of Hadar, Ethiopia on a long, hot morning of mapping and surveying for fossils decide, on the spur of the moment, to take an alternate route through a nearby gully, during which they spot a right proximal forearm, stop, and get out to look for more. They find an occipital bone, then a femur, some ribs, a pelvis, a lower jaw, and after sorting and screening and arranging hundreds of fragments of bone, assemble 40 percent of a hominid skeleton that would be named Lucy, once a member of a sexually dimorphic species known as *Australopithecus afarensis*, now a historic marker. I love her. She's my many times great grandmother. She's why I'm here. That and a huge mosaic of patterns and events, including a B-24 bomber, a mad German dictator with a short mustache, a redheaded woman from Denver meeting the pilot of the B-24, and hundreds of battles and castles and philosophies and civilizations, resulted in this, on these fingers typing this sentence and making a mosaic out of fragments of time and space and cracked perplexities.

I happened to bump into Virginia Woolf in the hallway to our building. I was coming out of the laundry room, where I noticed a mark on the wall. I asked her if she'd seen it. Yes, she had. She has many speculations on its origins, but nothing conclusive. I told her about a wall in a mailroom where I used to work, which was covered with all sorts of marks, presumably caused by all the mail hampers being shuffled about. It made me happy to look at because it reminded me a lot of Cy Twombly, an artist I very much admired. She was a Twombly enthusiast as well. I noticed she was wearing a pendant necklace with a stainless steel spider and asked if she liked spiders. Oh yes, she said. I love spiders. They're fascinating creatures. Their webs are so ingeniously contrived. I see them occasionally on the walkway, their thin, nearly invisible threads glistening with moisture. I told her we currently had a jumping spider as a resident in our apartment. She was living under the refrigerator, but lately seemed to be comfortable with us as she would come out and repose in the middle of our living room, which was a bit of a worry as we didn't want to step on her. Oriana found her in the kitchen sink this morning. She must've been thirsty. We were thinking of naming her, but we're not entirely sure of her gender. How do you tell if a spider is male or female? Look on the underside, if you can, she said, the female will have what is called an epigyne on the abdomen, which is an external sex organ. It's a little easier to identify a male as there will be two thickened pedipalps at the front of the head which resemble boxing gloves. I pondered this image, and envisioned myself getting into a ring with a feisty arachnid, a hairy Sylvester Stallone with eight eyes and several mean left hooks. Let me know what you discover, she said. Are you sure it's a jumping spider? They're more commonly found in Africa and Australia. Really? I said, a bit surprised. No, I confessed, not sure at all. Oriana has an app on her phone that identifies insects, but we're not very confident about its accuracy. Those apps are amazing, aren't they? she said. But you're right; a lot of these apps have bugs in them, no pun intended. I noticed, too, that Virginia was carrying a book. What are you reading, if you don't mind my asking? Oh, it's a really good book. It's called *Soviet Bus Stops*. I bought it for the daughter of a friend of mine who is fascinated by bus stops. There's a bus stop in Saransk, Russia, that's shaped like a light bulb, a big bulging structure with a large oval opening and a couple of benches inside. Is it lit from within? I asked. You know, I'm not sure, but wouldn't that be wonderful! It would be, I said. There's a bus stop in the U district near a bridge over the ship canal where I used to catch the bus to Capitol Hill. It was always dark there. One night a young man appeared holding a jar. He had a pet tarantula inside. He offered to take it out and show me, but I declined. The bus was about to appear. Juggling a tarantula could be awkward while trying to board a bus. Oh, but wouldn't that have been wonderful. I love tarantulas, she said. Me too, I answered. Well, I should be on my way and let you get back to your laundry.

Good talking to you, she added, and went on her way, her spider swinging from side to side. And let me know if you discover anything more about that mark on the wall!

It's 1.15 p.m. and I'm staring out the window at three soft shield ferns that are looking remarkably healthy. All of the plants in and around the apartment building are looking more robust than usual. I believe this is due to Oriana's recent retirement. She spends a lot more time with plant life, particularly the orchid she received as part of her retirement gifts, which were extraordinarily generous. The ferns are somewhat obscured by the grime on the window. It's a large double-paned window and we're unable to clean it. The immense amount of wildfire smoke from three seasons in a row somehow managed to seep into the space between the two panes of glass. The entire window would need to be removed. The smoke from those fires cast an apocalyptic gloom over the city on what otherwise would've been very sunny summery days in late August and early September. The smoke drifted into the city from three regions: Oregon and California to the south, British Columbia to the north, and the forests of the eastern Cascades to the east. It hung, asphyxiating and dirty, creating dangerously high levels of air pollution, for a week at a time, during which people were forced to stay indoors with their windows sealed shut. It was then that I began to realize how dire the situation is regarding the health of the planet and its biosphere. It's a feeling remarkably similar to those months and days when a parent or close friend is dying and the grieving process begins, slowly, incrementally, but also with a clear sense of inevitability and the knife-edge portent of extinction. If there are any extraterrestrials out there reading this, please, we need your help. We've learned our lesson. We promise to do better in future.

We head down to Lake Union to go for a run on Westlake,

past all the yacht marinas and houseboat communities and an ice cream parlor and law offices and cigar store and acupuncture and physical therapists and a scuba diving school and a beeswaxing salon and a ketamine clinic. This is a great place to run. The sidewalk is spacious and flat. The worst part is running under the Aurora Bridge. This is where a lot of the homeless find themselves, most often in tents, but sometimes with nothing for comfort or shelter other than the fentanyl or alcohol in their veins. I remember running under there last December when it was intensely cold and seeing the hulk of a man's body lying on the cement in a litter of broken glass and pigeon and rat feces without so much as a piece of cardboard to sleep on. I'd never seen such a grievous example of broken humanity.

I always think of my younger brother when I run down there. Somehow the starkness of the corporate buildings to the south of Lake Union, most of them the products of the technocratic juggernaut that exploded into world dominance, beginning in the late '90s, makes me think of him. He died in January, age 70, from a very sudden and unexpected illness called multiple myeloma. His body was wracked with pain in the final days before he passed. The hospital gave him pain medication but it had little effect. He begged for relief. A tumor had been discovered in his spine and he could no longer walk. He'd lost all feeling in his legs. One night he rolled over on his smartphone and "butt-called" me. He didn't talk. He wasn't conscious. I just heard his breathing, labored and heavy and spookily, mechanically rhythmic. Three days later he was dead. I used to call or write him to get his view on things when the world's bizarre developments and the predations of the so-called elites begged to be shared in conversation. Now, when I see those stark glass and steel buildings and their populations of silent zombie-like employees with their heads bowed as they go down the sidewalks, fixated on their phones, I think

immediately of calling him and sharing our state of alienation and unrest, before I realize he's gone. It's like having a
phantom limb, an amputated arm or leg whose sensations I
can still feel.

I wonder if we're trapped energies that rejoin all the other
energies and fuse with them to become one big energy-filling
space with radiant affirmation when we die and the body falls
from us like dead weight. These are the idlenesses of summer. The definitions of winter are hard and full of concision.
The shapes of summer are trees. Ramifications of sunlight.
Everything we find is handled like a story. A rock, a shell, a
cow's soft muzzle. Knowledge dies on paper. That prayer is
dazzling that prays to the bean and being and blackberry
alike. The Queen of Bohemia jumps onto an unknown pillow
on her bed. It's sausage night, get crazy. Chew the air like
meat. A mass of forest stamps wildly on the defeated world.
Words that are absent from themselves turn and roar with
color. I shall develop a barometer for that. The chasm calls
forth its equations and grounds everything in smashed limestone. The stake is moving, and the tent shakes.

We're treated once again to the Blue Angels rehearsing their
air maneuvers over the city in preparation for Seattle
Seafair. They're loud. It's exciting. Also baffling. Why military jets? F/A-18E Super Hornets, to be exact. It's a long tra-
dition. They began doing their air shows in 1946. It's a display of immense power and excites feelings of prowess and
dominance. I wonder if this is how the Vikings used to feel
as their long ships approached the coast of England. Blood-
lust. Berserker mayhem. The fury of steel. The roar of
dragons. Whooosh!!! go the jets, a roar so deep you can feel
it reverberate in your blood. Who wouldn't want to ride in
the cockpit of one of those hornets? The world and sky spinning with delirium as the plane goes through its maneuvers.
You've got to admire the poise and self-possession of the

pilots. It was, in fact, the pilot of a B-24 bomber that brought me into this world. I still have his Air Force jacket hanging in the closet, right next to the clothes I used to wear as a hippy in the late '60s. My frilly Regency shirt and Navy medical officer frock coat. My polka-dot pants and my Sgt Pepper ostrich plume.

I'm a biomass: that's how I've begun to think of myself in old age. A constellation of cells cohering around various needs, and an ongoing movie show in my brain in which I'm the star, an anti-hero, a doofus, an orchidaceous pirate, an astronaut of bubbles and sonnets, a vessel for the propagative forces of the language that inhabits me and uses me as its chief petty orifice, and a tinkly priest of all things tingly and daringly spurious. I dance whirligigs of maniacal glee to the sounds of Killing Joke's "I Am the Virus" and penetrate the zeitgeist with injections of Lear-like rage and madness. I am the virus. Spirit of outrage. I am the virus I am the virus I am the virus.

A beluga whale is swimming up the Seine. So far it has swum 63 miles inland. Means are being explored to feed it so that it will have enough strength to return to the open sea. This is a situation that has begun happening with increasing frequency. The animals appear to be disoriented by climate change and the underwater noise caused by humans and their machines. I'm reminded of the omens in Shakespeare's *Julius Caesar*, such as the lion Casca encounters near the Capitol or the ghosts Calpurnia sees walking through the streets of Rome before Caesar is assassinated. Or the visions of Cassius on his birthday just before the battle of Philippi, "Coming from Sardis, on our former ensign / Two mighty eagles fell – and there they perched, / Gorging and feeding from our soldiers' hands – / Who to Philippi here consorted us, / This morning are they fled away and gone, / And in the steads do ravens, crows, and kites / Fly o'er our heads and downward look on us / As we were sickly prey. Their shadows seem / A canopy most fatal, under which / Our army lies, ready to give up the ghost."

The whole world seems fraught with omens. Yesterday we saw a dead crow with its head torn off. Probably the victim of a raptor, owl or hawk. Still, it was touched with the ominous. Or weirdly dark mornings like today. So thickly overcast it's like night at 9:00 in the morning. And yesterday a man my age who cycles around the neighborhood and with whom I've developed a friendly relation stopped, ostensibly to say hello. I asked if he'd gone to France yet to visit his vineyard. Yes, he said, but he'd had to return because his son had been murdered. He'd been playing basketball at a court on Capitol Hill around midnight and an argument broke out and a man took out an AK-47 and shot him multiple times. He died of wounds to the chest. That's awful, I tell him. I was stunned, at a loss for further words. Another reminder of how bad the escalation of violence in the country is becoming. So yes, ominous, and then some.

It's 9.00 a.m. Mid-August. Very dark due to a heavily overcast sky. I hear the rain peppering the ground and leaves in little clicks and a soft murmur of air moving through the trees. I can feel it, too, a strong humidity suffusing everything. A strong cup of coffee on my desk. I'm reading *Hot, Cold, Heavy, Light*, a collection of art writings by Peter Schjeldahl. "But, because Picasso was an amateur – nearly a hobbyist – in sculpture," he states in "Picasso Sculpture" … "it revealed the core predilections of his genius starkly, without the dizzying subtleties of his painting but true to its essence." It's a stimulating book written in a prose that's alive and supple and describes artworks with such penetrating acuity and honest feeling it's like a sunrise in the mind.

I think a lot about libraries lately. Jerry Seinfeld's jokes about the ridiculousness of books and reading aren't help-ful. But it is, no doubt, the prevailing sentiment. Those of us who continue to read and write "literature" (pretentious word, I know, but what other can one use?) are like the monks at Lindisfarne. But it isn't Vikings we fear, it's Jerry Seinfeld.

There are currently 2.6 million libraries in the world. So somebody is doing some reading.

The world's oldest-known library – founded some time in the 7th century B.C. for the "royal contemplation" of the Assyrian ruler Ashurbanipal – is located in Nineveh in modern day Iraq and includes some 30,000 cuneiform tablets organized according to subject matter; tablets on divination, lexical, medical, mathematical and historical texts, legal documents, contracts, administrative texts, various omen reports, omen enquiries and their commentaries, as well as epics and myths such as the famous epic of Gilgamesh.

The world's oldest observatory is about 4,100 years old and was discovered in Shanxi Province, China. The remains consist of three semicircles made of rammed earth and thirteen stone pillars, each four meters tall, forming twelve gaps between them where people were able to view the shifting direction of sunrise and so distinguish the seasons of the year.

There's a modern-day functional Stonehenge in the Turtle Mountains of North Dakota. It distinguishes the winter and summer solstices and the fall and spring equinoxes through cuts in the stone measured exactly where the setting sun will be. The structure overlooks the prairie. I know the place well. My father designed it, though he didn't live long enough to see it built.

It's hard to conceive of the universe as having a beginning and an end. It just doesn't make sense. If it had a beginning, what was there before the universe? Space? Can't be. Space is a phenomenon created by the universe. It's a strange and invigorating thought experiment to conduct in one's head. Nice thing to do at an airport, waiting for your flight. Got to have a lot of coffee for that. Imagine a nothing that existed before something. But even that's impossible. Can't have nothing without something. Nothing without something is nothing. Absent something, you have nothing. Absent nothing, and you have ... what? Tickets to an ABBA concert in 1977? Those people sure liked to sparkle. Now they're performing as holograms. The public doesn't want to see old people. Me, I prefer the honesty of Keith Richards' face. And that hugely soulful version of "Time is on My Side" with Sarah Dash on vocals. Time is never on your side. This makes it a very odd and funny song. It seems to be premised on the idea that a lover who has rejected you will be coming back eventually, and that you can afford to wait. I can see that happening in a context of good times and getting involved in other things. Somebody with a healthy perspective on life. Or, as the undercurrent of sadness also makes clear, that person is deluding themselves. So it's not really a song so much as a short story. I've been there. I know the terrain, the smell, the sludge, the asymmetries. The stuck bureau drawers. The silly ivory knobs. The bottles of rum and whiskey on the coffee table. The incense and click of beads.

It's a warm Saturday afternoon, in the lower 70s, and we went for a run on Westlake again. The Blue Angels are out again and I can hear their roar, which is stunningly loud, but I can't see them. I feel a little cheated. The walkway along the big and little lakeside businesses is crowded. So are the bike lanes, upon which people on ebikes and escooters go tearing along at maniacal speed, the ebikers dressed in gear that looks like leftover costumes from a Mad Max movie, helmets and goggles and camouflaged army gear, death icons bearing the rictus of a lunatic devotion to Thanatos. Woe betide the pedestrian who wanders into their path. I wonder how many extra patients Harborview Hospital is getting due to the ebike and escooter craze.

"Have you seen the spider lately?" I ask Oriana. "No, I didn't see her this morning." It's odd, but I've begun to worry about this spider who has been with us for about a week now and has begun feeling so comfortable with us she'll sit out in the middle of the carpet in our living room. Even our cat leaves her alone.

"Here's an idea," I tell Oriana. "Somebody should start an Arachnid Magazine, with articles pertaining to everything arachnoidian: mating rituals, newly discovered species, impressive web designs, engineering feats, interactions with other species, that sort of thing. They could issue a calendar each year: spiders in bikinis, spiders dangling alluringly from their penthouse webs."

Later, while Oriana gets dinner ready, I watch an interview with French poet Christian Bobin on *La Grande Librairie*. I'm not familiar with his poetry, but I like what he says about books. He says a book is a little monastery that vibrates when it's well done and that our immersion in it links us to the entire world ... and that solitude is the perfect link to each living being in the world. Ironically, the Seinfeld episode we watch while we eat dinner a few minutes later concerns George Costanza and the extreme measures he takes to avoid reading a book on risk management for his job with the Yankees. He gets the idea of finding an audio version of the book so that he doesn't have to read it, but Jerry pops this bubble when he tells George that they don't make audio versions of textbooks. George finds himself sitting next to a blind man on the subway who is listening to an audio version of a textbook. Because there are audio versions of textbooks available for the blind, George visits an eye doctor under the pretense that his vision is so poor he's technically blind, hoping that he can get an audio version of the book on risk management.

I wonder what's at the center of the universe. A black hole? A 7-11? A John Deere dealership? A giant Cornish hen? A wormhole leading to another universe? A ripped old man pumping iron?

There's nothing at the center of the universe. The universe doesn't have a center. The universe doesn't rotate, so there's no center of rotation. The universe is infinite and uniform, so there is no center of mass because all points are identical. The charge distribution of the universe is infinite and uniform, so there is no center of charge. I find this disappointing. There's no place to take my complaints.

But wait a minute, you say, I thought the universe is expanding. Isn't it like a balloon speckled with stars on the surface expanding outward equally in all directions from a center within the balloon? Apparently not. The universe is expanding equally in all directions, but the directions don't have a center. All points in space are getting uniformly distant from all other points in space at the same time. Space itself is expanding. But what about the Big Bang? The Big Bang was everywhere in the universe and not at a single point. We see the flash of the Big Bang – cosmic background radiation – as coming equally from all points in space. The flash of light is equally strong in all directions. I find this dizzying. It's like being in downtown Manhattan for the first time with everyone hurrying in multiple directions. There's no one special place where any of these people are going. Ultimately, they all end up at the place they were going, wherever that is, since I don't know any of these people or where exactly they believed they were going.

The Making of Americans by Gertrude Stein is a universe of words with no center. That's why there's no future or past, no linear progression leading to a marriage or a divorce, no turned tables, no plot devices or witty contrivances, but a constantly expanding continuous present.

I envy people who believe in an afterlife. How is that not enviable? You die, you find yourself in a paradisiacal realm with all your favorite friends and family members, reunited with pets, a chance to meet God (the ultimate celebrity) who probably plays guitar better than anybody, even Hendrix, and why shouldn't he or she or it or they or we? She or he or it or they or we invented music. She or he or it or they or we invented pronouns, too. There are more pronouns available than anyone ever dreamt of. Pronouns for jungles of tropical reproductive strategies, including masturbation and asexual reproduction, and life forms not even imagined whose single organisms have multiple reproductive organs, enough to fill an afternoon with the wildest pornography anyone has ever seen.

I've often tried to imagine what life would be like without a body. A sense of selfhood in what I can only imagine would be a nebulous ectoplasmic mass of energy. Or would it be more like Swedenborg confidently espoused an afterlife would be like: essentially the same stuff and same arrangements we have here, but going on forever. I'm not sure that's all that attractive. Swedenborg was a mining engineer. I met a lot of engineers via my father, who was in aerospace. They're an odd bunch. You think poets are weird? Go have coffee with an engineer.

And then there are astrophysicists. An astrophysicist might tell you that gravity is always attractive and never repulsive.

That's wrong. Ask a mountaineer who has just fallen from a cliff. They're not going to tell you gravity was so very pretty as they plummeted to the ground.

I'd say gravity is a force I've learned to live with, like most people. I love space. I can't say enough good things about space. And gravy. Gravy is fantastic. But gravity, not so much. I'm sure I'd appreciate it more if I spent six months in the international space station. Astronauts sleep in a sleeping bag with a rigid cushion that exerts pressure on the back and gives the impression of a mattress, even when floating. They look like cocoons but with their head and arms exposed. I wonder if anyone has attempted to have sexual intercourse in weightless conditions. Things could get awkward. Sex is awkward enough as it is. But one mis-judged thrust could send you and your partner spinning madly around the capsule, arms flailing, the romance gone.

I've been around the sun 75 times and I still have a lot of questions. What is the meaning of life, and why do people get so upset when you bring it up? Why is work so inher-ently unpleasant? Who invented the desk? Do ghosts really look like bedsheets? How does superman manage to fly without any evident means of propulsion? Is human con-sciousness an epiphenomenon, something without a direct function, like the redness of blood, or more like an emul-sion, a light-sensitive coating on photographic film? How does neural activity become a subjective experience? Is there intelligent life elsewhere in space? Is there a parallel universe where people walk on the ceiling and poetry is the highest paid profession? Who wrote *The Book of Love,* and where can I get a copy?

Things turn spectral around midnight. Here comes William Shakespeare riding a language. He'll tell us. He'll write a play that asks everything and explains nothing, and for that we will be glad and toss our hats in the air and praise the new king and feel aggrieved for Falstaff.

Rhyme is like a venereal disease. This is how I came to sing at Covent Gardens. To destroy rhyme with a jarring, discordant, asymmetrical song. But I traded my speaker for a bike. And can't sing anything without a mic. Just remember one thing: time is on my side. At least I think it is. It's an odd thing to declare at my age, but there it is, a drippy clepsydra, also called a water clock. I'm reaching out now, reaching out to feed my mind. It's hungry. Hungry for answers. Hungry for olive trees and rubbery succulence. For gems of intellectual distinction. And nothingness. Nothingness most of all. Cool blue nothingness.

Certain people seem drawn to oblivion. They become estranged from the world of routine and structure, ancient mariners like Coleridge's grey-bearded loon and glittering eye.

I continue to find it remarkable that Danny Kirwan wound up homeless on the streets of London. His music was so ethereal, and he a rock and roll Pre-Raphaelite with an angelic look. And the group itself seemed to be pretty popular at the time. Wouldn't that have resulted in a fairly secure income with royalties coming in for at least another 20 years or so from record sales, not to mention CDs? Nirvana became extremely wealthy on the merit of a few albums, not many more than the ones Fleetwood Mac produced before morphing into an ultra-popular group once Stevie Nicks and Lindsey Buckingham joined the line-up. That was long after Peter Green and Kirwan parted ways. Green, too, became homeless for a time, psychotic, it appears, from a horrific LSD experience. How strange all that is. A tragic story. With dimensions awash in uneasy gouache.

I ask Oriana who that songwriter is she likes so much, I can't remember his name. Nick Drake, she tells me. She describes his music as sad and wistful and recommends that I listen to a song called "River Man." Which I do. His voice is smooth and soft and the melody has a nice easy flow to it. The lyrics are evocative but simple, permeated through and through with the wandering idleness of a day in late spring, when the world's demands are far away and the more tangible mysteries of life's pulses and pulls are at play. Betty, the central figure of the song, appears to be in quest of the healing properties of nature and its unbounded distance from pain. The river man is mythical, or real, the shaman of a local village, maybe. He's got the answers, though nothing is specifically addressed; this is a song, not a short story, so everything stays beautifully vague the way they do in songs where the music carries the feeling and the words seem to drift through like harmless pellets of sound. Drake, another doomed romantic, like Kirwan, died at age 26, a year older than Keats, of an overdose of amitriptyline, an antidepressant.

The world is very different to the one I remember from the 1970s. Democracy still had something of a kick to it, electoral politics still managed to effect good progressive change despite the evident corruption metastasizing in the body politic. We inhabit a very different planet now.

I've grown accustomed to a world in which my life and the lives of millions of others are dependent on the behavior of idiots. The most recent example being president pro tempore Flora Ferrari's jaw-droppingly reckless and stupid trip to Taiwan to thumb her nose at the China. The government of the State of New York ran an ad, just a few days before this event, giving advice on what to do if there's a nuclear strike. This included taking a shower and laundering one's clothes. But how does one take a shower if one has been vaporized? And what would be the point of clothes?

Early in the movie *Twelve O'Clock High*, General Savage (Gregory Peck) informs a roomful of trained WWII bomber pilots about to engage in their first missions that they would do well to consider themselves already dead. The survival rate for WWII bomber crews flying missions over Germany was nothing short of abysmal. It's a grim but serviceable mindset to get into. To adopt. To adapt. To force oneself to inhabit. I'm not sure I could do it. Though, at age 75, maybe I already have.

There's a Buddhist tale about a monk and a teacup which may or may not be apocryphal, the gist of which is that the teacup is no ordinary teacup but extraordinarily beautiful, which elicits a response from the monk's guest who asks if the monk isn't nervous about sipping tea from such a precious vessel. The monk answers that the teacup is already broken. It's a lesson of non-attachment: if you assume that what you currently love, enjoy, appreciate or even worship is already gone, then you're in a position to truly enjoy that ephemeral being or object. Internet trolls love debunking these offerings, but I still like it. I find it helpful.

I remember the Cuban missile crisis of 1962. I was a sophomore in high school, living in a suburb of Denver, Colorado. I remember my classmates sitting outside at a picnic table joking about the whole thing. The idea that we could get blown up at any minute inspired a weird hilarity, a gallows humor. It was then that I realized that this teacup planet we inhabit is already broken, already gone. All the tornadoes, hurricanes, heatwaves, droughts, floods, the melting ice cap and glaciers, avalanches, even earthquakes and volcanic eruptions, are caused by an abrupt change in climate that is the result of carbon emissions baked into the atmosphere from 40 years ago. All this talk about what we should do to save our planet is sheer vanity. What we should've been for decades is building cisterns and aqueducts and replenishing forests rather than destroying them for real estate developments and the perpetuation of cheeseburgers.

Rumors abound that the HNWIs (high net worth individuals) are building underground bunkers to ride out the apocalypse when the rest of us are shriveling up like bean pods on the hot unlivable surface. These will be underground shelters made from military-grade materials that will provide protection from nuclear war and/or a chemical attack while remaining cyber and pandemic secure. Most will include food supplies for a year or more and be supplemented with hydroponic gardens. Some will even include space for a small community, replete with a theater, classrooms, a medical clinic, a spa and a gym. A sniper tower on the surface will provide a little added security if life on the surface goes completely Mad Max. Some companies already investing in this area recommend that owners commission the same builders and designers that worked on their yachts. Some will even include a pool, general store, bar, library, and wine vault. All this while the not-so-fortunate will be eating one another's brains. Food for thought.

OK, that last bit is a bit snarky. I know. I can't help it. I find the rich disgusting. They didn't used to be. Remember Margaret Dumont in the Marx Brothers movies? She was buffoonish in her pretensions and gowns and pearl necklaces. There was something vulnerable about her, too. And Harpo chased silly debutantes around on a bike, tooting a silly horn. It seemed that the rich still had some measure of humanity. At some point they became starkly, unmitigatingly psychopathic. They exploited us lesser humans for what remained of our resources, our energy, our passive adaptability. *My Man Godfrey*, with William Powell and Carole Lombard, which came out in 1936, begins with a group of wealthy individuals in a whimsical scavenger party. One of the "items" they're seeking is a "forgotten man." That's how they come to discover Godfrey (William Powell), living with other unemployed and homeless men at a New York City dump in a Hooverville, on the East River. That world bears an uncanny resemblance to the one we're currently living in, the one exception being that the homeless population has grown exponentially and their encampments are everywhere, under bridges, in vacant lots, on construction sites and sidewalks. Why no one has thought to bring out a remake of this movie is mindboggling. It's timely and, sad to say, timeless.

The wealthy socialites in *My Man Godfrey* weren't entirely inhuman, as becomes apparent as the plot unfolds. I'm not sure you can say that about today's wealthy socialites and technocratic elite, the Kings and Queens of Silicon Valley, the nabobs of Wall Street, the chichi real estate tycoons, the Hollywood celebrities and politicians and the Jeffrey Epsteins that feed on their depravity. These people are craven in ways that bear more predatory resemblance to the slimy alien of Ridley Scott's movie. Minus the narcissism, of course. That may be their one humanizing quality: vanity. It's thanks to them that we have a thriving nail salon industry.

But who am I to make these judgments? Wouldn't I behave much the same if I had a lot of money?

I need a more sobering perspective, a broader outlook. I need to find a more neutral zone to inhabit. I'm not fighting any battles. I haven't marched in a protest since 2003, when Oriana and I joined a few hundred people in a walk around Greenlake holding candles to protest the imminent war in Iraq, while UW frat boys shouted epithets from their Escalades and Hummers.

Spinning my wheels. That's all I seem to do. Maybe it's time to leave the car behind and walk the rest of the way.

To see what has not been seen until now by leaving oneself behind. How can that be accomplished?

Strip the old man, as Saint Paul would say. It's a question of forgetting oneself in one's own present in order to try to spot the needs in others. If you want to see into history, you have to strip yourself of all preconceptions. It's not a comfortable process, but there's something exquisite in this kind of pain, this kind of discomfort. As soon as something is removed, other things rush in to take its place, the unknown mixed with the unexpected. History is a journey outside of time. When people travel, they don't expect to find the same reality in other countries. It can be stressful, always feeling awkward and trying to adapt, but the stimulation is worth every bumbling moment. It's that much harder when one is dealing with one's interior being and feeling disoriented by new perceptions. This genre of travel isn't as easy as linking to a map on Google or getting on a plane. There's nobody to stamp your passport. Hard to even get it going. Where does one begin? It's one of the central reasons people have begun experimenting with hallucinogens like DMT again. The French have a word for it: *dépaysement*. Outside one's habits and the familiar.

People are siloed. Specialists do not communicate with other specialists. Knowledge isn't shared, because it's been commodified. It's all about profit. This started before the pandemic, when smartphones displaced conversation. And the chatter of the weeklies. People can no longer speak to each other as we spoke to each other when we all had more or less the same limited knowledge, and the conversation took us to places we didn't expect, and gave us ideas we wouldn't have thought up on our own. Now there's an intolerance of ideas different or contrary to our own. It's what killed the coffeehouse. Not to mention conversation.

And yes, I get accused of being overly negative all the time. But here's the deal: you need a negative to get a picture. I live in a culture that frowns on negativity, but the focus on positivity is far more toxic. Glibness and denial are the hobgoblins of the human condition. They present themselves as helpful and benign when they're anything but. They place scales on your eyes.

I'm living on a planet that's already gone. I keep searching for a clue, inkling, sign, omen, anything that might indicate a more benign future. I listen to climate scientists on YouTube. I read books on climate science and reports on the coral and phytoplankton and forests and hydrological cycles, trying to get a toehold on an outlook that includes life in all its guises and forms. I take an avid interest in the health of the world's colleges and universities and academic conferences, assuming they survive the current disease of censorship and repression and return to the more invigorating pursuit of open inquiry.

I know it's there – something I'm not seeing. Some invisible force, power, agency, dynamo or 11th hour fleet of extraterrestrial ships filled with wise sapient beings that will use their knowledge and superior technology to give life on this planet another chance. Some people will say "God. God will come. God will save us." Ok, I'm not going to argue with that, how could I? It's a matter of faith. That said, how do you know all this doom and gloom isn't part of a celestial plan? A purgative. A cleansing. Remember Noah? I'll bet he spent a lot of time at Home Depot.

Is it any wonder that a few of the billionaires want to get off the planet completely and set up a new civilization on Mars or Titan? Is Elon Musk the new Noah? I don't think so. It may be presumptuous of me, but I don't see Mr Musk including everything from prehistoric nematode worms living in arctic permafrost to box huckleberry to blue whales in the cargo holds of his magnificent spaceships. I just don't.

It almost seems more viable to wish for supernatural intervention, i.e. a deafening crack of thunder followed by a giant hand reaching down and sweeping over the oceans and continents with a healing power, before receding into the sky, leaving everyone stunned into silence, while birds resume chirping and dogs bark just like they do after a solar eclipse. Would that do it? Would that get people's attention? Would it serve to pry their eyes away from their phones?

God? Yes, maybe. Wouldn't that be spectacular? In the meantime we have GAD. Generalized Anxiety Disorder. A lot of that going around. But is that level of daily anxiety really a disorder? How is it a disorder? Disorder suggests a malfunctioning. But anxiety isn't a malfunction, it's a state of alertness. If you're a small but tasty mammal living in the Cretaceous, surrounded on all sides by hungry reptiles, many of them big as cars, a state of alertness helps to keep you alive long enough to reproduce and care for your progeny. Oriana and I have no progeny. We were somewhat beyond our reproductive years when we met. We care for a cat. We feed crows.

Sunday, August 7th, 10.30 a.m. Oriana returns from her walk with a photo of a Persian silk tree, a very rare tree for the Pacific Northwest. It's in the yard of a house on a quiet residential street with an unusual number of crows. No idea why there are so many crows on that particular street, it's pretty much like all the other streets. There's one crow in particular among this bunch who's a real crab. He's very aggressive when he wants a peanut. You'll feel the rush of air from his wings as he brushes over a shoulder, or thumps your head.

Our spider friend died this morning. Oriana found her body under her chair, little legs curled up.

"She's gone" – Hall and Oates, 1973. *Cash Box* described the song as "starting out softly, the build is strong with super strings in the background to tie the package together." "Super strings?" Superstring theory posits that the universe exists in 10 dimensions simultaneously. Hall and Oates posit that everybody's high on consolation. I agree. Consolation sucks.

It's sunny and hot. We do the Westlake run again. It's not very crowded. Most of the city has gone to the south end of Lake Washington to watch the hydroplane races. The Blue Angels fly overhead, shredding the inner organs of my ears. I look up to see three jets in tight Delta Formation, shaping an arrow: another reminder of what a militarized death cult this country has become. We stop at a public dock to gaze out over the water. There are a lot of people enjoying the lake in kayaks and paddle boards and small sailing boats. We hear the scruffy sound of a rope being pulled through a hole on the upper hull of a yacht being moored to the dock. Oriana tells me there are dragonflies here. There are a few metal plaques attached to the upper railing of the dock which has been angled slightly to make it easier to read them. All of them are anecdotal aperçus of life in and around Lake Union. One of them concerns a boat named Elsie:

> I found her up in Marysville in the mudflats
> with water running in and out of her, and I
> fixed her up. She had been a rum runner, a

patrol boat, a dental missionary boat, and a
lovely brothel in southeast Alaska. Everywhere I went oldtimers would say is that
Elsie? – Dick Miller

We peer into the water. I love the way sunlight refracts and
shimmers in the water. All those oscillations are mesmerizing, transfixing. I wonder how long I could stare at it
without getting bored, or remove my shoes and jump into it.
Dive down and shake hands with a mermaid. And sure
enough, there are a number of dragonflies hovering and
dashing over the waves. Their bodies are blue, same color as
the Blue Angels, but they tend to be much quieter.

Later in the evening, while listening to Sophie Hunger's version of "*Le vent nous portera*," I finish reading *Where Are
We Now?* by Giorgio Agamben, and am moved by the con-
cluding words:

> What is happening today on a global scale
> is certainly the end of a world. But it is not
> – as it is for those who are trying to govern
> in accordance with their own interests – an
> end in the sense of being a transition to a
> world that is better suited to the needs of
> the human consortium ... We are not await-
> ing either a new god or a new human being.
> We rather seek, here and now, among the
> ruins around us, a humbler, simpler form
> of life. We know that such a life is not a
> mirage, because we have memories and
> experiences of it – even if, inside and out-
> side of ourselves, opposing forces are
> always pushing it back into oblivion.

Also available from grand**IOTA**

Production of this book has been made possible with the help of the following individuals and organisations who subscribed in advance:

Rosa Ainley

Christopher Beckett

Paul Bream

Andrew Brewerton

Ian Brinton

Jasper Brinton

Peter Brown

Allen Fisher

Giles Goodland

Penelope Grossi

Randolph Healy

Lindsay Hill

Kristoffer Jacobson

Sharon Kivland

Don Lawson

Heller Levinson

Richard Makin

Michael Mann

Shelby Matthews

Peter Middleton

Paul Nightingale

Sean Pemberton

Lou Rowan

Alan Singer

Carol Watts

www.grandiota.co.uk

www.ingramcontent.com/pod-product-compliance
Lightning Source LLC
Chambersburg PA
CBHW020649260626
47157CB00008B/2965